City of Masks

Mike Reeves-McMillan graduated from Auckland University in New Zealand with a Master of Arts in English language and has worked as a book editor, technical writer, corporate trainer and systems analyst. He is currently establishing a practice as a hypnotherapist.

City of Masks is his first published novel.

City of Masks

Mike Reeves-McMillan

www.csidemedia.com

Dedicated to my late father, who taught me to be an
honest man.

Private journal of Darion, Lord Rivers, Under-secretary to the Foreign Minister of Calaria

The sixth of the first month.

Perhaps I might soon enjoy relations with my wife again.

Sir Willard Chase, that good man, is dead – and I mourn him as is proper. But with his death there comes available a post to which I may appoint Gregorius Bass, so that my honoured spouse may be reconciled to me.

It always astounds me that a woman otherwise astute should so romanticise such a one as Gregorius, half-brother or no. True, he bears a strong physical resemblance to their late father, and has even many of the old man's mannerisms. This circumstance has deceived others, myself included, though never for so long as it has deceived her. Their father was no fool; a badger of a man, black and white, solid and slow-moving, tenacious, fierce when cornered, but no fool.

True, also, that Gregorius is some years older than his sister, and she has often told me stories of how he was her hero and her protector when she was very young, and he not yet away to school. (I sometimes think that if I hear the tale of how he rescued her from the millrace once more, I shall not be responsible for my actions.)

It passes my belief, however, that she thinks him a brilliant prodigy, unfairly held back by his relationship to me; when in fact the exact opposite is the truth.

Many have been our late-night arguments, Katara insisting that he ought to be given a position more suited to his talents; I (having been a diplomat) forbearing to retort that I can hardly demote him, but protesting that I cannot be seen to be nepotistic. She, that surely all know his ability. I, again diplomatic, that no suitable position is available. She, to sulks; and I, alone to a cold bed.

Now, though, with the death of Sir Willard, Bonvidaeo has fallen vacant – a sinecure, made for a plodder, a clod, a filler of forms, a seat-warmer such as Gregorius. Almost a ceremonial post, a hangover from an earlier age, a token to prop the pride of a few Calarian mercers and fullers in that now peaceful city who, since the time of my predecessor's predecessor, have not required the services of an envoy for anything more than permits and official seals – the issuance of which is well within even Gregorius's competence. I believe there is even a book which sets out the procedures, written in a fit of boredom or zeal by some previous incumbent and handed down ever since. He can read, even if slowly, and it is not a long book.

"Envoy" as a title has a good ring. I think Katara may be satisfied with "envoy".

My only concern is that he may offend the odd customs of the Bonvidaeoans, and to that end I asked Tailor, through whose ears all knowledge passes, to search for some native of that city to serve him in the capacity of guide. Gregorius is looking for a new valet (he bored me almost senseless the other night with a long tale about how the present fellow can never heat his shaving water to the right temperature), so I can foist one upon him and not seem a meddler. Indeed, I shall be the solicitous brother-in-law.

Luck was mine again, for Tailor stated immediately that he knew of such a one; a youth, trained to service in one of the great houses of Bonvidaeo, who had sought adventure as a sailor, landed here for a season, and now desired to return to his native country.

(If only I could appoint Tailor to some post fitting to his worth! But were he not a commoner, or were he posted out of kingdom, he could not serve me by the wealth of contacts and the knowledge of the deep currents of the city that he has. I must be content with paying him a clear crown higher than his official post should merit. Had I but more Tailors and fewer Basses...)

The seventh of the first month.

The sun shines upon me, though outdoors it is winter and the trees display no leaves. I enjoy, again, the favour of my wife; and find myself much relaxed, and in good temper with the universe.

Today, also, I have met the Bonvidaeoan youth. He is a slender fellow, quick of movement, speech, and thought, and mature for his years, which number perhaps eighteen or twenty. He has the foibles of the Bonvidaoans: will not look one in the face, and wears the mask all his countrymen affect; yet his tact would not disgrace a man of my own profession. He is educated, he tells me, in the lore of masks of which that City makes so much, and will be able to serve as clerk and secretary in addition to his valet duties.

He strikes me as the ideal guide for Gregorius. I cannot imagine a youth more suited to keeping a fool out of trouble.

Private Journal of Gregorius Bass, Envoy of Calaria to the City-State of Bonvidaeo

The twentieth of the first month

The sailing from Calaria has been good, the weather fine, the salt breezes refreshing and the motion of the ship pleasant. I am in excellent health and spirits.

This day we sighted the low, wooded headland which, when rounded, brings us within sight of Bonvidaeo. Accordingly, we shall be required to don our masks shortly to comply with the Bonvidaeoan law. Although a low fog hovers around the point and we will probably not be literally visible from the city – and certainly our faces will be not – Corius says that this is not what is important.

Corius, whom His Lordship so thoughtfully provided as my valet – after I mentioned in passing that I was dissatisfied with the last man – Corius has been telling me at length of the origin of the Bonvidaeoan customs, and as it is a droll story I shall record it here.

Some three hundred years gone, it seems, Emilion, first of that name, was king in Bonvidaeo. This Emilion was much addicted to the fantasies and foibles which occurred during the season of Carnival, which then was, as in all the countries around, a matter of a week. This decadent obsession, along with the bibbing of much wine, inclined the monarch – whose power at that time was absolute – to extend the period, first by another week; then, when that week was almost ended, by a month; and then, when that month was almost passed – making six weeks in all – did he declare, and have passed into the city-state's ordinances, that Carnival would run year-long.

His high ministers threw their full support behind this novel law. Corius would have it that they looked for His Majesty's distraction with the entertainments of the Carnival, not for a week, but perpetually, to allow power to descend to their own shoulders; but Corius is something of a cynic. The merchants, who made their best money during Carnival, were also disinclined to oppose its extension, though in fact their annual income rose but little – for it was the special nature of the time, and not the festivities alone, which encouraged free spending.

From the religious arm, there was at first opposition, for Carnival fosters that wildness which in Tolland they call "maskfreedom". Revelers, their identities concealed, play their tricks and japes with impunity, and license prevails, against the teachings of religion. But it happened (perhaps by coincidence, though Corius hinted not) that the then Archpriest died shortly after the edict, and his successor convened a Council of theological reasoners and logic-choppers to study the matter. After being closeted for almost two months, they emerged with the basis of a new doctrine which has prevailed, except for certain heretics, since that day.

Worship in Bonvidaeo, and indeed surrounding nations, has always involved the use of masks to depict the presence of the gods among men; and Carnival, too, involved the secular use of masks to represent famous characters, mythological and historical.

What the assembled theologians birthed, influenced (says Corius) by certain cunning factions among the King's ministers, was the doctrine of Characterism, which was always (they claimed) inherent in their belief and practice. This doctrine holds that *the mask is the thing*. That is to say, a priest in the mask of the god is the god, standing among his worshippers, a legitimate focus of awe and adoration. Likewise – and here is where the ministers benefited – a man in a mask of a mythical hero is that hero.

Thus the ministers, small men in truth, could glorify themselves by adopting the masks of famous wise men, statesmen and saviours of their nations; and the Bonvidaeoan religion now required the orthodox *to treat these men as those men*.

Heaven be thanked, we have no such custom or belief. But the Bonvidaeoans, who have maintained and sophisticated this doctrine over time, make it the basis of their very society, and so I must go masked to move among them or be guilty at once of a sin and a crime.

Though the other aspects of Carnival are no longer practiced in Bonvidaeo to any greater degree than in other nations, this masking continues in all places even theoretically within sight of the City, as I have alluded to already. Corius, good servant that he is, has prepared for me several masks – for the making of masks is a skill prized by Bonvidaeoans, and he has made a special study thereof with an elderly savant of his acquaintance.

When I am in my official capacity, I must mask as an Envoy, while at other times Corius thinks it safest, until I learn the customs, that I be Uncast. This means a simple black robe and domino, and so long as I do nothing to draw attention to myself nor do not seem to be in any character, I am effectively invisible, protected from harassment by any passer-by. (For some of the masks are malign, and some have complex traditions attached to them; and if I gave the wrong response to one such while in a character, I would be denounced as Unmasked and vilified at once as a criminal, a blasphemer and a transgressor of etiquette. For religion, law and social mores all agree in Bonvidaeo – at least touching the matter of masks, though perhaps less so on other matters.)

When we reach the city, Corius says, he will take me to consult his former mentor, the elderly and respected Felkior, who keeps the Book of Masks. This important ceremonial post is given to one wise in history, myth and the lore of the mask, and on his advice many trials, civil and ecclesiastical, are settled. For it is he who records, and recalls, the meaning, form, and legends of the various masks, and how the characters depicted by them should act, and who is licensed to wear which; so Corius hopes that this sage (of whom he speaks as fondly as of a father) will be able to find for me some inoffensive persona in which I can safely move about in Bonvidaeoan society.

Far from feeling threatened by the risk, my blood is thrilled. It is an adventure that My Lord has given me; and I feel at once like a discoverer of strange lands, and like a maiden at – as it were – her first masked ball.

We are about to round the headland, and I must mask.

The twenty-first of the first month

I write this in our inn, a fair enough hostelry in the clothmakers' quarter (and thus in proximity to our office), whitewashed within and without and furnished with the angular, solid furniture of the last century. It was as well I had Corius with me, for when we entered the inn, the innkeeper no more took notice of me than I had been the air itself. Corius, good fellow, was masked as a Servant, and as such negotiated our rooms. But I was Uncast, and according to the very law of the city, invisible.

I asked my servant as we ascended if any ever make use of the mask of the Uncast in order to commit crimes. Certainly, he said. But if they are caught, then they are charged not only with one crime – whether it be theft, murder, assault – but with the far more serious crime of being Unmasked.

You could, he said (addressing me) have sat upon any of the chairs or at any of the tables; placed a coin upon the bar, and received ale in exchange (for to exchange ale for coin is proper to a Barman, and no matter that no man is seen to give the coin or take the ale); taken a coin to the servery and received food in exchange, for the same is proper to a Cook as is proper to a Barman; warmed yourself at the fire, if you obstructed no man else; and none would have spoken to you, or of you. If the City Watch came and inquired of you when you were gone, the Lord Justice himself, if he were present, would swear there had been no man seen, and not account himself a perjurer. But if you so much as took a mouthful of another man's soup, or tripped him as he walked to the door, every man in the room would seize you, and hale you to the officers for Unmasked.

It seems, then, that I am safe enough, and can carry on my life in peace, if I trouble no man and take pains to behave as if I am invisible. The disadvantage is that they will all treat me as invisible also. I will have no impact, no significance. To a nature such as mine, this is abhorrent, but it must be bourne with until we can find me a mask that will enable me to walk abroad without imperiling the grave mission entrusted to me, that of representing my homeland in this foreign place.

Today we went in search of a house to rent during my tenure here. As Corius explained, it must appear suitable to my station; and so we searched in the great streets and the wide.

Houses here are not as houses at home. At home, any apartment which the inhabitants are wont to use must be comfortable and reflect such style and status as the owner has. Here, this is true only of the rooms seen by visitors; and these are furnished lavishly, at the expense of the rest of the house. I have strayed sometimes into servants' quarters and onto servants' stairs in the houses of the wealthy, through having missed my way, and have known it immediately by the poverty of the decoration compared with the pomp of the other rooms. Well, here the contrast is much greater, and only a couple of rooms are decorated up; the rest are bare and chill, that more may be spent on those which guests shall see.

The fronts of the houses, too, are most lavish. The streets they give upon are broad, as I have said, and used only for carriages and sedan chairs. Carts and the like use the back streets; and they are truly back streets, for they run behind the houses, and are mean and narrow in the extreme, and often set lower than the main streets. Many of the greater thoroughfares have tunnels plunging beneath them to carry the common traffic, so that not even the exit of what is called a "street of the second city" is seen to open upon them. Like the Uncast, they are conventionally invisible. A third network rises above, the High Paths – bridges and walkways strung from roof to roof, upon which only the upper classes may walk. The wealthiest and most powerful live in the upper stories, above the residences of their dependents and supporters; they are the upper classes in literal truth.

The houses of the poor in our city are clustered meanly together in one quarter; in Bonvidaeo, the poor are one's neighbors, but neighbors one never sees. They live off the alleys which run behind the houses of the rich. Nobody has back windows here, or back doors either, except what let onto loading docks for supplies. A few of the greater houses relegate even these to their cellars; the palace, for example, is surrounded on all sides by broad ways, down which carts are forbidden from moving, and is provisioned from a network of tunnels below ground, suitably defended.

All this Corius told me; I did not see the mean streets for myself, as he thought it inadvisable. We have found one or two fine dwellings – fine in outward appearance, that is, and Corius says that this is all that matters – and we will look again tomorrow.

Tomorrow, also, or the day after, Corius hopes to take me to Felkior, an introduction to which I look forward with eager anticipation.

The twenty-third of the first month

I must, before my memory of the day's events fades, commit them to paper, for they are curious in the extreme.

Yesterday we spent as the previous day, searching for a house; we settled at last on one, on the corner of Weaver-Street and the Ribbonway, and we will be removing there before many more days, after which I will present my credentials at Court. Corius has commissioned from a tailor whom he knows a suitable costume for an Envoy, and has himself made a mask for me.

This mask he showed, as if for approval, to Felkior at our interview today – for today, at last, I met that remarkable and most redoubtable old man. The sage inspected it carefully with his long, slender fingers, not once glancing at it, and for the first time – we had been there some quarter of an hour – I realised that he was blind.

"Yes, young man," his amanuensis, one Tamas, whispered to me; "had you not known?"

I am scarcely now a *young* man, for I am four-and-thirty; but Tamas is older by twenty years, and I forgave him it.

"Known what?" put in the sage, sharply; and I swear his eyes were focussed on me. I could tell the direction of his eyes better than with most Bonvidaeoans, for he wears a peculiar mask, granted to him... but I am not telling my story in order.

We arrived at the house – which is not ostentatious, a pleasant stone house with bright rugs, which it now occurs to me must be for Tamas's pleasure, as his master cannot perceive them – we arrived, I say, in the mid-morning, and grey-haired, grey-robed Tamas opened to us. Corius knows the secretary well, and introduced us, and we ascended to the old man's study. This is a chaos of volumes, crammed on shelves, scattered on tables, all centering about the great Book which is Felkior's charge, the Book of Masks. Masks, too, there are in great profusion, many of them attached to the bookshelves or suspended from the ceiling, others forming place-markers in books or intermingled with them on the tables and desks, cloth masks, papier-mâché masks, leather masks, feather masks, a carnival in miniature around the cluttered workroom of the scribe.

The old philosopher himself wears a singular mask which covers only half his face. It is, moreover, a mask *of* his face, which is a thin, intelligent physiognomy with a hook of a nose above a white goat's beard. However, it represents this face when it was somewhat younger and less wrinkled; and in the course of the conversation he indicated that this was an honour awarded him first in his youth, when he gained distinction as a living Character.

"For all our masks," he said, in a voice surprising deep for one of his age and thin frame, "are based on some Character or another, whether of myth, or legend, or common tales, or a stereotype of one's occupation such as the Secretary portrayed by my friend or the Servant portrayed by your young fellow here, or the Envoy which he has rendered with some skill. (A lighter hand with the sequins might perhaps have been in better taste, but no matter. Provided they are silver and not gold...? Even so. I should have trusted you to remember.)

"Sometimes, you see, a person becomes a legend – or a myth, or a common tale – in their own lifetime, and then they are themselves classed as a Character. See here," he rose smoothly, smoother than I would have predicted from his lined face, and striding to the table of the great book, located one bookmark of many by the feel of the ribbon, and opening the volume indicated an entry high on the right-hand folio.

"Here is the description of my first Character, which I won in my misspent youth." I bent beside him to read it, and could make little sense of the glyphs and abbreviations in a kinked and crabbed hand.

Seeing my puzzlement, the secretary stepped to my aid, and recited in an even tone something like the following:

"FELKIOR. Accepted as a Character on [the exact date escapes me, but it was some years before my own birth]. Age 19. Of the class Lover, the subclass Philanderer, the type Successful, the subtype Unrepentant. Characteristics: athletic, daring, wild, contemptuous, amoral, flippant. Approach: dazzlement. Secondarily of the class Swordsman, the subclass Rapier, the type Excellent, the subtype Flashy. Characteristics: wounds, does not kill unless hard-pressed. Approach: out of the sight of women, strikes quickly and accurately, does not fence; in the sight of women, will fence impressively unless in danger of capture. Thirdly of the class Dandy, the subclass Fashion Leader, the type Daring, the subtype Tasteful. Characteristics: bright, but not gaudy, primary colours, subtly combined, innovatively cut. Approach: innovates at each social event. Mask: black silk half-vizard, deep red silken band with many golden broken hearts across the forehead; four crossed rapier symbols spaced evenly across the centre of the mask, made of steel, painted in red, blue, green and yellow; a fifth, steel, unpainted and un-paired rapier offset out of pattern on the left; along the bottom of the mask, stitching of ribbons of the same colours, inclined to the right, not in a regular pattern of colour or any two of the same width."

I cannot say my puzzlement decreased; rather, it grew greater as I looked at the elderly, scholarly gentleman before me, whose white mask was of cloth, but not silk, and covered half his face, but not the upper half (it was the right). It was not that of a youth, but a man in middle age, and the silken band across the forehead might once have been pale pink but now looked al-most white. The symbols he bore were six, and were tiny scrolls – actual scrolls, they were three-dimensional, not painted, but tied on with little cords – and the bottom of the mask had reg-ular stitching of sober grey ribbon, inclined to neither left nor right. The only colour was a small feather, like a peacock feather, hanging by each ear.

"My second character," said Felkior, "was much different." Without having to be prompted, the secretary flipped to a later page in the huge volume, and read another description. This one matched the man and the mask I saw before me, and other than that I cannot recall it accurately – I was still somewhat struggling with the previous characterisation.

"You see," the scholar said when his assistant finished, "there have been two characters called Felkior."

"That is one way to put it," said the secretary.

"Well, how would you put it?" his employer demanded.

"That you, Felkior, have lived two different kinds of life in one lifetime."

"Twisting, twisting, always twisting!" cried the old man – though he did not appear angry; indeed, he was grinning even as he remonstrated with his amanuensis, gesturing with a wrinkled finger.

"I could say the same," retorted Tamas.

"Not so; it is a valid viewpoint. You said as much yourself."

"And you believe that because it is a valid viewpoint it is true."

"And you believe that because another viewpoint is true, this one cannot be true also."

"And you..."

"Gentles, gentles!" put in my servant hastily. Both men looked a little shamefaced; their debate had rapidly grown loud.

"My apologies, Mysir Bass," said the scholar. "Tamas and I are old friends, and old debating partners with it; we hold differing views on some points of philosophy with which you should not be wearied."

The secretary made his apologies also, and I accepted both, of course. Then we proceeded to the main purpose of my visit: to identify a character I could safely assume within Bonvidaeoan society.

"Tell us of yourself, then, Mysir Bass," invited Tamas.

"Tell us," said the scholar, "of who you would wish to be." I thought another debate was about to break out, but the blind man glared – precisely at his secretary, too – and the man subsided. I thought myself that Secretary Tamas took too much upon himself.

"Well," said I, "I have always been a physically strong man, though I am not quick. I am, I hope, a man of honour; I am industrious, and I think reliable. I am not cunning, and dislike cunning men. Apart from that I know of no virtues I possess, save loyalty."

"My master is too modest," said Corius; "he is also a courageous and courteous man, gentle to his friends, fierce to his foes, and generous to those less fortunate."

I stared in some surprise at my servant, for I had not expected his tribute, especially on such short acquaintance.

"And how," I asked, "did you reach these great conclusions?" I may have spoken a little sharply, for I was unused to such forwardness in a servant; yet I was complimented.

"Mysir," he said, "tell me if it is not so."

"It is true," I said, "that I have no fear of man, beast, or natural force, beyond what is prudent and necessary; that I keep the ways of my gentle ancestors in these decayed times; that I am not a man to frustrate; and that I sometimes give trifles to those in need. But how had you concluded this on such a short acquaintance?"

"I must confess," he said, "to having spoken somewhat with Tailor, Milord Rivers' assistant, and he gave me some such a word-picture of you. Also, I am an observer of mankind, and of human nature, and having watched you, I know his words are true."

"But how, when you have not seen me at any risk, nor speaking to a friend, nor confronting a foe, nor – as far as I recall – giving alms?"

"As to giving alms, there was a beggar this morning," he said; "we were talking at the time, and you did not seem to remark him, but you gave to him – a silver coin, I saw it flash – without pausing in your speech."

"You are right," said I; "I had forgotten it."

"As for the rest," said Corius, "a man is all of a piece; to see one thing in him is to see all. And many small words and actions of yours point to the truth of Tailor's saying."

Now truly, I had never thought Tailor a particular friend of mine, or an admirer; almost the opposite at times, I had reckoned; but I can admit when I am wrong, and I owe the good fellow an apology, I see now. I shall do somewhat for him when I am next at home.

We talked for some time longer, and then Corius fell to suggesting with the old man and his secretary masks that might fit me; as, "Gentle Knight", and they murmured, "No, for we want no provocation"; and "Honest Courtier", and they said, "No, too rare, too obscure; and there are risks attached to that one, which you may not be aware of"; and some more I have forgotten. Often, Felkior and his secretary fell to arguing some point of philosophy, and Corius had to return them to the topic. Their talk was filled with many terms and references which I knew not, being foreign, and I was soon lost. I had ceased to attend, and was watching the passing traffic from the window (for none of the sage's many books looked light or amusing), when one of them – Tamas, I think – cried, "Of course. The Innocent Man."

I turned around – for his voice had been loud – and surprised an odd expression on the face of Corius, which changed, however, in an instant; it had looked like amusement, but what with the mask it is always hard to tell expressions, and it may well have been rejoicing only.

"Aye," said my servant, "the Innocent Man. Ideal in every way."

"It is true," I said, "that I am guilty of no wrongdoing; but what is this 'innocent man'?"

"The Innocent Man," explained the sage, "is a mask worn rarely, for it is rare, as you know, to find a man without any guile at all. Its significance is this: that any question asked by the character is to be taken, not as a veiled insult or intended blasphemy, even if such is the plain meaning of it, but as the question of an uninformed innocent who means no harm thereby.

"The Innocent Man has no enemies, for he offends nobody. He is openhearted and generous. It is always wrong, and always an offence, to challenge him, or to attack him; he should be protected, rather. The only thing is this, that he is not known for courage (though he is not known for cowardice; the Innocent Man is simply not placed in situations which require courage), and he is not unusually courteous – not so as to be remarkable for it."

"We always thought," said Corius, "that three or even four masks might be needed. How is this: The Innocent Man for daily wear or when in social situations; the Envoy for official occasions and for courtesy; and perhaps the Gentle Knight for courage, if it is required?"

"You have your heart set on the Gentle Knight, do you not?" asked Tamas, smiling.

"Well, and why not?" asked the sage his master. "It is a good mask. Scriven out the descriptions, then, Tamas, in plain language so that our client can read them, and Corius will be a good fellow and prepare the masks. The Innocent Man is simple – a white sheep's wool domino with wide eyes and raised eyebrows; and the Gentle Knight – ah, I grow old, Tamas, and there has not been a Gentle Knight in some time; copy it out, man, and read it to me as you do so."

The secretary did so, but he had gone no more than four words into the description when his master's voice joined him, and completed it without his help, needing only the jog to his memory. The Gentle Knight is portrayed with a half-vizard mask of soft sky-blue-dyed leather, and a sheathed sword at either side is bound to a peacock-feather; the other details I cannot now call to mind.

"It is a feather-mask, being a mask of war," said Corius; "that is good."

"What is a feather-mask?" I asked.

"You must have seen the feathers in the masks of the city watch, between the eyes?" he replied. "They were once real peacock feathers – am I not correct, Master?" (addressing Felkior, who nodded as one pleased with an apt pupil), "but an enterprising rogue held all the peacocks in the city to ransom, and it was declared that any feather dyed with the eye pattern of the peacock would suffice. They symbolise the all-seeing eye, you see, and anyone who wears one can perceive even the invisible characters, like the Uncast."

"But surely anyone can perceive them," I said.

"Now that," said Tamas when they had all finished laughing, "is a remark of the Innocent Man."

"But I am Uncast here, and you can see me," I protested; "I am not really invisible."

"No, but you are conventionally invisible, which is just as good, or better, because if you bump into a table nobody will pay any mind, unless you spill or break something. And as for being visible here – my Master is the Keeper of the Book, and all characters are an open book to him, even the Uncast, and he wears peacock feathers by his ears to symbolise this – that he can see them, as it were, with his ears. And I am his Secretary, and it is proper to a Secretary to perceive what his master knows."

I was silent at this, astounded at their convoluted logic. It is true that in this city I am an innocent, and could wish for no better mask than the Innocent Man.

We had risen to depart when came a pounding on the outer door, which gave out on the street a floor below. Corius, to spare the Secretary, descended the stairs in his headlong manner, and opened to a winded messenger. Descending more slowly after the youth, Felkior demanded what the matter was, and I heard the gasped words clearly from the stairwell.

"My master – sent me to say – the Keeper should know – the Butcher's mask has – been stolen from his rooms."

I saw the secretary, who was standing in the doorway, clutch at the doorframe in an access of emotion.

"What is it?" I asked him in a low voice.

"The Butcher," he said, "was a notorious murderer who was executed some years ago. He is a Character who is never portrayed and there is no official mask, but a death mask was taken. The messenger is a servant of a noted collector of masks, in whose collection the death mask – reposed."

"But reposes no longer?"

"It would seem not. And I fear there could only be one reason to take the mask. Some person wishes to portray this murderer, and his bloody crimes will come among us once again."

The twenty-sixth of the first month

I have spent the last two days in great busyness at our small office, ordering all to my satisfaction and catching up upon the applications which have languished in the absence of an envoy. Two weeks' worth of applications, however, is not seemingly a great many, for with Corius's able help I finished the last this morning and we had little to do this afternoon.

I have come to regard him greatly and rely upon him, for he is a youth of great capacity, helpfulness and resource. He has also a pleasant personality, though he takes morose moods from time to time; yet he is always polite and deferential to me and to those who visit the office, and takes pains to help them beyond what most clerks would trouble themselves to. His advice is always good, and I have cured him at last of diffidence in offering it.

We spoke at some length this afternoon, and told each other of our histories as friends newly acquainted might do, rather than as master and man. He has two sisters, he tells me, Juliana who is his twin, and Sallia who is the same age but a foster-sister. His mother Mende raised them all without a husband, as a servant in one of the great houses here. No wonder that he is so fine a servant, for he has been trained to it from birth. His loyalty, too, is bred in, for he said his mother is a cripple, injured in an attack on her employer. He himself grew restless in the great house, and sought a different scene to play out his life in – as they say here; taking service as a sailmaker, he sailed upon a merchant out of Tolland, first to that nearby land and then to my own Calaria. He missed his home, however, and found the nautical life less congenial than the service he had been raised in. Inquiring for passage back to his own city, he encountered Tailor, who referred him to My Lord and he to me.

I, in turn, told him of my late parents, my older brother who has now the estate, and my younger half-sister, who is married to My Lord. It was a pleasant time; I warm to him, and he I think to me.

We went tonight to see the old men, for Corius resorts to their company frequently and they welcome him more as a favourite son than as a student. They welcomed me also, and I was led to reflect that in my own country, where men show their faces, I am "that plump fool Bass" and no man's friend, but here in the City of Masks I have three friends and am just myself. Despite the strangeness of this place, I think I can be happy here.

To Court tomorrow, so I must to sleep now.

The twenty-seventh of the first month

Today I was received at Court, with all honour due to a representative of our great nation. My impressions of the event are vivid and I hasten to set them down.

The Palace is surrounded by wide avenues, almost like squares in their extent, and here are many heroic statues, fountains and the like, and lantern-posts which are lit at night. They shine upon stone walls of impressive height and in good repair, behind which the Palace presents a spectacle of elaborate carving and decoration such as is usually confined to temples in our more restrained northern lands.

We arrived in a hired carriage (for I could not afford to own one of such magnificence, and Corius advised me that magnificence was required), drawn by three matched pairs of greys; I, costumed lavishly in scarlet and gold as an Envoy, and with my Envoy's mask in place. The tailor, by the way, had taken a leaf from his neighbor the carpenter's book, and placed a fine veneer over lesser stuff, to reduce the cost; the outer layers were silk, but the lining such coarse, unbleached linen as a carter would disdain. This, I am told, is the common fashion of the place, and only Lovers, who look to have others see beneath their garments, wear silk and the like next to the skin.

Corius attended me, in the sober costume of a Secretary which he had borrowed of old Tamas. I had desired that he might accompany me to instruct me on points of etiquette, for truly they were too many for my poor memory.

The Palace is of considerable size, and of as great magnificence within as without, with marble and gold leaf displayed everywhere (though Corius, always wishing, it seems, to reduce my wonder, whispered that the marble was as thin as they might make it, and covered common brick). Rich carpets of the South are on the floors of the grand corridors, and a multitude of lamps burn in crystal shades, illuminating the way we trod to the hall of estate.

To cover my nervousness and make conversation, I asked my good attendant, "Tell me, this King Emilion; he must be from ninth or tenth of that name?"

"Nay," he whispered, as one shocked; "this is Emilion the First."

"But how can..." I began, for I knew that Emilion the First flourished three centuries ago.

"Shhh," he said, "you are not presently the Innocent Man. He wears the mask of Emilion; therefore, he is Emilion, and all Emilions are one Emilion, the first of that name."

I was silent, and risked no more questions, lest the guards hear and hale me to justice as Unmasked.

The court was of great splendour, as I was by now expecting. Every conceivable surface shone with gold, or rather, with gilding, and the nobility in attendance on the king were a very flowerbed. High windows let in the sunlight, and at every turn it sparked off jewels – on hands, on clothing, and above all on masks. The courtiers' masks were fully elaborate, encrusted with gold and silver and gems, thick with symbols, bedecked with sigils and signs. An ornate and byzantine courtesy rules their every interaction, says Corius, and it is a game that admits no new players, for the rules are not written as are the rules of masks. They are passed verbally from father to child, from mother to daughter. "Like a guild," I said to him, and I thought he would injure his stomach. He is often morose, my Corius, but when he laughs he laughs heartily (though with a voice something high); and when he recovered his breath, he bade me not make that comparison in the hearing of the nobility. (As if I would! Condemn me if he do not at times take on more the character of a nursemaid than a valet.)

But I wander. All that was later. At the court, I received, and returned, bows from many courtiers, friendly enough in intent, I thought, though Corius says all part of the game.

At last, after walking what seemed an avenue of flowering trees to one with my slight affliction of the sight, but was merely a congeries of courtiers either side a Southron carpet, I bowed before the king, Emilion the First as I must style him.

It was here I perceived the spring and origin of the ornamental dress affected by all at court. I do not wish to speak disrespectfully of the king of a country where I have the honour to be an emissary, but His Grace is of middle height and something thickset, and wears a robe of such gorgeousness and size that I can resemble him to nothing so much as those flamboyant birds which one sometimes sees brought from the jungles of far lands. His mask is a miracle of gilded intricacy, more architecture or sculpture than clothing. It seems that it attempts to represent the feats of both the king himself and his distinguished ancestors, but at a length and in a style and a symbolic language that conveys nothing to me, a foreigner.

The herald who had accompanied us announced my name and station, I bowed deeply, the king nodded to me very slightly, and the audience was over. I was led off again to a side room where a small collation was laid, and Corius whispered, "That was the show – now for the real thing."

Before I could ask him what he meant, the first of a long train of courtiers seemingly happened to appear at my elbow and spoke to me of matters that for the most part I knew not of. I answered him politely, and at length he disappeared with a small bow and an excuse, at which juncture another replaced him.

And so it went. I never saw a man of them hover (or a woman, for some were women – I will tell of one momentarily). Never did they seem to be waiting to see me. And yet, the moment one left, another came, as if at an unseen signal. According to Corius, this was exactly what was exchanged, but they are so subtle that he cannot read them and can detect them only rarely. "Then how know you that the signal exists?" "By logic, sir, for they could not do it without a signal."

Corius is a great devotee of logic, having been trained in it by two philosophers, old Felkior and his secretary. Sometimes I think he makes a god of it – and like any man with his god, invokes it whenever he is confused or frightened.

There is one woman I specially marked, out of all that river of faces (or rather masks), each different and yet with such a sameness that none other of them was memorable. She wore a mask of masks – covering half her face (the left), though seemingly shaped to it, but made up of tiny masks carved in many materials, laid on so thickly that she had semblance to a victim of the plague whose face had broken out in boils. Yet her figure, as could be told by the elaborate gown she wore as much to show it as to hide it, was slender and youthful, and her voice was low, rich and thrilling. I took note of her at once and started from my stupor of ennui and confusion.

We talked for several minutes, then she, too, departed, and was not replaced – she was the last, seemingly, though I would have remembered her had she come in the midst. "Who was that last woman?" I asked my servant as the herald led us back to the conveyance.

"That," he said, something tightly, "was the Countess."

"Just 'the Countess'?" I queried him.

"That is identification enough for any in the City," he replied; "though others here hold that rank, she is *the* Countess. She is one of the Commissioners of Masks, as her mask of masks portrays."

I started to ask another question about her, but he hushed me, saying that it was not thought proper to discuss a lady where one could be overheard.

As the carriage was hired, he kept this silence all the way back to the residence. There he unburdened himself of what seemed a long bitterness.

"I did not dare to say this in the Palace, or in the carriage," he said – his voice hushed even in our own rented house, but forceful as I had not heard him – "but the Countess is the most dangerous and vicious woman in this dangerous, vicious city, even among the nobility, who make the starving rats in the sewers look like models of ethics, compassion and gentle dealing."

I began to protest, but he would not be silenced. "She is a snake, Mysir, a scorpion, and if I could be sure to grind her underfoot I would take her sting in a moment – and there are many would take my body up and bury me in a hero's grave for the service done the City. Stay clear of her, for your life and sanity. She holds more power than any man in Bonvidaeo, the king not excepted, and she uses it with a cold ruthlessness that would blench you to behold."

"More powerful than the king? Is she his – his leman, then, the power behind the throne?"

"If the king has not had her it is a mark of distinction in him, for she has the morals of a cat as well as the claws and the compassion. But nay, she is not his leman or any man's. She is the unofficial but acknowledged chief of the Commissioners of Masks, and they hold the true power in the city. They control the King, the Council and the priests, who all are puppets which mouth their sayings; and as the City is to the Commission, the Commission is to the Countess. You have met the ruler of the City this day, Mysir; and what is less, you also have met the King."

The twenty-eighth of the first month

Corius has his holiday this afternoon, so I am here in the office alone. He goes to see his family in the City, as a good son and brother. I gave him leave if he wished to have his family come to our house, for which he thanked me courteously.

He is a great assistance to me in the work of the office here also, and in teaching me of the practices and ways of the City. Our small office has little business, on some days none at all, and we have determined to use the time in study. He has been well educated, if informally, by the two old men, and he is teaching me to read the Book of Masks – the lesser edition, based on the great tome in Felkior's study – for, he says, I must know at least the common masks if I am to get along here. I cannot hide always behind the ignorance of the Innocent Man.

It is difficult study; I have always found bookwork uncongenial, as I am more a man of action than of scholarship, and I said to him today that it seemed the book was written so as to make it harder to understand than it needed. He said, yes, it was. I often do not know whether he jests, or what his jests mean if he does so. But he must often recall my attention to the book; any drifting speck of dust draws my eye away, or some person passing in the street. He uses these latter to drill me, asking me to identify each occupation or place in life. Because of our location, I now can tell a milliner from a mercer from a dyer from a weaver with some facility, though many others pass whom I cannot yet identify. Corius sketches well, and besides the masks that pass the windows he has shown me some of the more important or dangerous masks with a few strokes of a quill upon the back of an old piece of paper. I begin to feel that had I lived my entire life to date in the City, still I would not have mastered the lore of masks. Corius, however, says that all learners feel so at first and I will soon know the symbols like a native. He is a good and patient teacher, and appears to enjoy spending time even with such a dull and inattentive pupil as myself.

I am writing this to distract myself from studying in the Book, so I ought to stop. But I must first record my thoughts about the Court yesterday and our conversation this morning.

"Surely," I said, "you exaggerated the power of the Countess to me yesterday. One woman, of such relatively low rank, cannot be the effective ruler of the City as you suggest."

"Indeed she is," he said, "by cunning and manipulation and setting one group against another. You will not find her name among the high officers of state; but when she appeared one day at the meeting of the Royal Council, which feigns to govern in the King's name, none dared exclude her – or so it is rumoured. Nor is she the nominal head of that Council, but I have heard that he who is the head looks for her nod from the corner of his eye before he rules on any action. He fears to do otherwise, for accidents happen to those by whom the Countess is annoyed, while those who do her bidding find themselves advanced in the world."

"But surely this is all rumour and hearsay," I cried.

"Mysir, it is breathless whispers in the dark inside thick walls," he replied – and indeed he had kept to a low voice for his accusations. "To say a word against the Countess is not considered – healthful."

It all seems very exaggerated to me.

Ah, well, I should I suppose to study, lest I treat a Minister of State as an idle fop or the other way about.

(Later) It is dull here without Corius, and I can study no more; my head is on the point of aching. I wish something would happen in this wretched city in which I could take an interest.

Private Journal of Sallia

Not dated

Today Corius came to see us and Juliana of course and it was very merry for a time but then Mama and him got in an argument because he said the Countess had tried her wiles on the Envoy the man he works for and mama said what wiles do not speak of the countess that way and he just sighed and said nothing. I think mamas leg is hurting her it is always worse when it is damp and then she gets angry and Corius has no patience. Then they started back through all their old arguments and he drew me in and tried to make me take his side and I would not. Just as well Bardo came and we all pretended to be not arguing. Bardo has not met Corius before and I do not think they trust each other they are like a pair of cockrels walking around each other deciding if they will jump and start fighting. Mama likes him though you can tell but she took some of her medicine and it makes her go odd and I had to put her to bed. I told Bardo when Corius had gone that he could trust him he has odd ideas but he is all right really. He said what sort of ideas. I said he does not like the aristocrats and the government and the temple or any of that. Bardo laughed and said it sounded like they had things in common and I said I do not like you to talk that way because it scares me. But then he become lovy as I had hoped and we did not talk about Corius or politics anymore it was good.

Private Journal of Gregorius Bass

The first of the second month

My hand shakes and my pen scratches and blots – I can hardly write, for there has been a tragedy. Today early at our office Corius was just opening the book to drill me at masks when a weeping woman of Calaria, masked and costumed as a Mercer, burst through the portal with her hair and clothing in disarray. Corius, good fellow, seated her and went to get drink while I attempted to calm her sufficiently to ascertain her need. "Good woman," I said, "you are with friends. Now, has someone of this city attacked you? Should I send my man in pursuit?"

She wept and gasped, but could not speak. Then came a grim man, a Mercer also but of Bonvidaeo, and at first I feared that this was her assailant, but he crouched beside her and spoke to her gently, then looked at me with eyes of pain. "My partner," he said, "her husband – he has been horribly murdered in the night. They are of your country so she ran here for help. The guards are not interested in the death of a foreigner."

Corius returned just at this juncture and inquired urgently, "Murdered? Murdered how?"

The man glanced at the weeping woman and forebore to answer in words, lest he distress her further perhaps. His eyes were cast down and seemed to look on a distant – and horrible – scene.

"It is near our shop," he said, "and we all reside above. I must take her home – her daughter can take care of her. Can you accompany us?"

We shut up the office and hurried to the mercers' district – nearby, for our office is located in the same section of the city as those I serve. The woman was handed off to her red-eyed daughter and the partner took us through the shop to the sunken alley at the back.

This was my first sight of the Back Ways, as they are known, at least among the polite (there are other, more opprobrious terms, I am given to understand). Being below the level of the main streets, so that they can pass thereunder without intruding upon the promenade of the gentle, they are drains for all manner of filth and offal – though better so than as it is in our own country where this same office is served by the gutters of the main streets themselves. The stench was indescribable, but was made far worse than usual by the corpse of the unfortunate mercer, a plump man of middle age – at least, by his clothing he had been plump, and by his wife middle-aged, for he was in such a condition...

It is difficult to write of this. The murderer had opened him in the manner of eviscerating a beast for eating, and blood was thick upon the...

His inward parts had been removed, and...

The murderer had made a mask for him of his own intestines.

I am not ashamed to say that I did not long retain my breakfast. My good servant was as white as a girl who sees a serpent. The partner bowed his head in sorrow.

At length Corius spoke. "We must move the poor fellow. We cannot leave him – like this."

"Yes," I said, "we must. Good mercer, we must bespeak a bolt of your cloth – thick canvas, if you have it. We will wrap him."

"We should first return his... we should restore him to..." said Corius, and broke off, retching.

"I will do that," said I, "for I have been a huntsman, and with such scenes – though not involving persons – I do not completely lack acquaintance. If you would be so good as to procure me gloves," I added, looking at the state of the mercer's sadly defiled corpus.

During the grim operation I noted that the head was loose upon its neck, as if it had been broken. I drew this to Corius's attention and asked him what he concluded.

"That the man was killed first," he said, "and... the other treatment given him afterwards."

"Yes, and that explains why, although there is much blood, it is all close to the body, for dead bodies bleed more sluggishly than live ones," said I. "I wonder why he was murdered in such a manner?"

"The proximate reason," said Corius, "would seem to be that the murderer could therefore be less besmeared with blood, and so escape notice more readily. At least, that would be the likely reason except for one thing."

"What is that thing?" I asked him.

"That the murderer would have been in the costume of a butcher, and so to be besmeared with blood would be proper to that costume."

"How do you know his costume?" I asked.

"You recall the messenger, almost a week ago? The one who reported the theft of the mask?"

"The mask? The mask of – do you say that this is…"

"Aye, Mysir, this murder has been done in the manner of the Butcher. The exact manner down to every detail."

The second of the second month

Corius is absent today upon a commission to speak with certain of his contacts in the City, that they might assist us in investigating this hideous murder. I understood from his comments that they are not necessarily such persons as should be officially known to be visiting the Envoy of a foreign power. Strange that a youth of such upright character should have contacts who are criminals, but in this city criminality has at times a definition which I do not understand. Everything in this city has such a definition, it seems to me at times, and this is such a time.

As little as I wish it I must write a dispatch to My Lord and also an official letter to the authorities here, laying out the circumstances and requesting their assistance. I hold out more hope from Corius's criminals than from the keepers of the law, nevertheless. My observation is that they are unwilling to stir a step without a bribe and give a sneer only in return.

Dispatch from Gregorius Bass, Calarian Envoy to Bonvidaeo; to Darion, Lord Rivers, Undersecretary to the Foreign Minister of Calaria

The second of the second month

My Lord, it is my great regret to report a monstrous murder in the City, of one of our own Calarian citizens.

The citizen concerned is an honest mercer, by name Colmus Weaver. He was found by his servant in the alley which runs behind his dwelling and shop, murdered and mutilated in a shocking manner. His household attest to the character of the servant and state moreover that the lad was under their eye moments before the discovery. Footprints of the murderer, much larger than the feet of the servant, were visible coming and going in the alley, so the lad is comprehensively cleared. Besides which he is a small lad and would probably not have the strength to perform the act.

The rest of the household swear to each other's movements and also do not match the footprints.

Colmus Weaver leaves a wife and two daughters and his death is widely regretted by Bonvidaeoans of the cloth trade and expatriate Calarians alike. The man was not in debt nor was there any other reason known that he might have been murdered. The Calarian community in the city is nervous and I have received today many petitions for protection, which I am at a loss to provide, having no forces at my command and no wherewithal to hire any. I have advised our citizens to secure their homes, to travel in company and to remain alert but calm. It is not my belief that the man was murdered because of his nationality and I have declared this repeatedly to all who come to me. Currently it appears that he was the random victim of a lunatic, though almost certainly a native Bonvidaeoan.

I am doing what I may to mobilize the forces of the City in pursuit of the murderer. I would appreciate your Lordship's support in any way that you might contrive.

With much regret at having such sad news to report to Your Lordship,

I remain,

Your servant,

Bass.

Official letter to Commander of the City Guard, Bonvidaeo; from Gregorius Bass, Envoy of Calaria

The second of the second month

My most respected Captain Portavin,

I beg leave to draw your attention to a situation of concern to all residents within the city of Bonvidaeo. Yestermorning was found, in the mercers' quarter, the corpus of Colmus Weaver, an honest tradesman of my nation Calaria. He had been most viciously murdered and mutilated in a very shocking manner, his entrails having been removed from their proper place and arranged upon his features in the manner of a mask.

Naturally this circumstance has caused great concern within the whole Calarian community and indeed among the mercers and fullers generally, as he was well-known and well-regarded in these trades.

I ask most respectfully that you assign some capable men to seek the murderer, and also to patrol the quarter concerned. In the anticipation that this will put you to some administrative inconvenience I enclose a small remittance to offset any expense to which this matter may subject you, and add to it my thanks in advance for your attention to this matter.

In anticipation of your speedy response, I remain,

Yours respectfully,

Gregorius Bass, Accredited Envoy of the Lion Court of Calaria to the City-State of Bonvidaeo.

Private Journal of Gregorius Bass

The third of the second month

After closing the office today I sent Corius to confer with his associates and went myself to the old men, for I had remembered the fencing prowess of Felkior in his youth and wished to consult him. I am a fair fencer but notable more for strength than for skill, and hoped that he could assist me in improving my ability in case I was subjected to attack.

"Indeed," the old sage lectured, "it is only in that case that you should use these skills, and only if you are masked as the Gentle Knight. The Innocent Man is never attacked and need not defend, and the Gentle Knight ignores all taunts and challenges, but will defend himself if directly attacked – or defend others if they are directly attacked. And by 'directly' is meant 'with physical weapons', not with words."

"I have never paid great attention to those who strike with words," said I, "for they cannot harm me. If I could not ignore an insult I had been dead or a criminal ere this – for in Calaria, dueling is illegal."

"Here it is, for some characters, almost a legal requirement," replied Felkior. "Well, then; mask as the Gentle Knight, remove, if you would be so good, your shirt, and stand you up to my good Tamas, for he was almost my equal in his time."

"Remove my shirt?" I asked. "Is this another custom?"

"Nay, not of the city," he said, "but how shall I know your stance except I put my hand upon the muscles of your back?"

I had once again forgotten his blindness. The sensitivity of his other senses appeared to compensate, for he could, indeed, tell my stance through "reading" the muscles of my back, as Tamas and I worked through parries and ripostes. Before long I was glad of my shirtless state, for Tamas was quick, and I in a sweat, though we kept our feet unmoving – "bladework before footwork" was Felkior's training method, and it enabled him also to keep his hands in contact.

"You are strong," said Felkior when we paused, "but not quick. Therefore, a solid defence is the first thing to achieve, and then the art of binding the other's blade to disarm. The Gentle Knight prefers to disarm rather than wound."

"Indeed," I replied, "so do I." This almost provoked a debate over philosophy between the two old men, but they restrained themselves for my sake. We lit lamps then, for the darkness was closing in.

We worked for some time more and then rested; I had resumed my garments and was taking refreshment when there came a pounding at the door. Tamas hurried to open, and was almost knocked prostrate by the incursion of Corius, who was weeping and almost incoherent.

"Corius," I cried, "what is the matter?"

"Another murder," he sobbed. "The Butcher. And – the victim – "

He broke down and could not continue until calmed by Tamas. At last he whispered:

"My mother."

Tamas blenched and sank trembling into a chair, releasing the elbow of the weeping youth. "Mende?" he said. "Mende has been murdered?"

Corius nodded, unable to speak.

"Mende," muttered Tamas. His master, who had been pouring a tumbler of spirit for Corius, poured a second for him and brought it, and he gulped at it distractedly and then swore as the rough drink burned in his throat. Corius sipped his more cautiously and sank also into a chair. The old philosopher paused a moment and then returned to his cabinet and poured two further tumblers, for me and for himself. Their colour matched the lamplight in the room, I noticed with the irrelevance that one is subject to at such times.

"Did you – know Corius's mother?" I at last asked Tamas cautiously.

"In my youth," he began, then fell silent and looked at Felkior.

"Tell him," said the blind man, seeming somehow to detect his gaze.

Tamas turned, not to me, but to Corius and said gently, "You are my son."

Shocked from his grief, Corius stared at him.

"We had agreed never to speak of it while we both lived. But also, we had agreed to tell you should one of us die, so that you would know."

"Could that be...?" Corius breathed as if to himself.

"What is it?" asked Tamas.

"She spoke the other day of a secret that she wished to have written – nay, but it must have been something else, for when I suggested she come to you, that you would write it and keep her confidence, she said 'I know. He has never told...' and stopped. She..." He sat suddenly upright. "She must have decided to come to you. That must have been where she was going. She was murdered between the Countess's residence and here."

I must have appeared puzzled – no, I must have made a puzzled noise, for Felkior, sitting beside me, leaned over and said quietly, "Mende was formerly lady's maid to the Countess. Her foster-daughter Sallia now fills that role."

"The Countess? Then you were raised in her house?" I asked Corius. He nodded.

Suddenly his warnings about the Countess took on a new authority.

We all fell silent with our various thoughts, then Tamas, shaking himself, asked, "Can you remember her exact words? When she was speaking of the secret?"

Corius leaned back with his eyes closed.

"She had taken some of her medicine – for the pain in her leg. I think perhaps the medicine – it is strong. She talked more freely after taking it, with less sense, but still holding back her secret. She said she wished she could write, and I offered to write for her if she wished, but she said she must not tell me. She said if anything happened – those were her words – she wanted it written. She said she thought she was close, that she thought she knew."

"Close to what? Knew what?"

"She did not say. Would not say. I suggested coming to you. She agreed that you would keep a confidence. She said you were a priest, and when I said 'No longer' she said aye, a priest of the Moon, and you had never told... She stopped. I said, priests of the Moon are women. She insisted that you were one, though you would deny it. I asked if she would go to you and she said aye, another day, when her leg was not so bad. It should be written, she said again, in case. Then she took more medicine and it put her to sleep."

He stared into the distance, remembering. Tamas frowned.

"I am not a priest. No longer. In my youth," he explained to me, "I was a priest of the Sun. But that was taken from me, and as Corius says – priests of the Moon are women. And illegal," he added.

"Tell them the truth, Tamas," said the old scholar. "Bass can be trusted."

"Well – they offered to make me a priest. But I set conditions they could not well meet."

"He told them that he would become a Moonpriest on the day that they made a woman Priest of the Sun."

I thought that Tamas would glare at his friend for this speaking out, but he only fixed his eyes upon the table before him.

"My mother said you would deny it," said Corius quietly.

"Then your mother was right," he said, not quite shortly, "for I do deny it. Not to protect myself, for I do trust all here, but because it is not so."

"I think I understand," I said. "I think she meant that a priest is not what you are made by men – or women – it is what you are. A priest is a holy man – or woman – who portrays the god. And though no man nor woman calls you priest, yet priest you are, and always will be priest if you are a holy man who portrays your god." There was a silence, then:

"The Innocent Man has spoken," said Tamas, "most holy, most heretical. Rank Personalism which would see any other tied to the post and whipped by every passer-by in the Great Square. It is as well we are friends here, Mysir, for you are wearing the wrong mask. But you are correct. Men gave me a priesthood when it meant nothing to me, then denied my priesthood just when it had become real. Not for my beliefs, though that was the reason given, but because I would not look aside while they told lies to the people."

"Because you were a holy man," Felkior said, "who portrays the god."

"I would not say so much. But we digress. What are we to do? How shall we avenge Mende, find this murderer?"

"My foster-sister Sallia," said Corius – "her lover Bardo is – he has, let us say, access to resources. I did not dare ask him over the Calarian, for his concerns are within the city and are not – "

"Do not wind yourself in your words," said Felkior. "He is a leader of the underground, yes?"

"Aye. I believe his devotion to Sallia is genuine and besides, this threat affects us all. He will help."

"My people of the Moon are pacifists, those I trust at least," said Tamas. "But they can watch, and they pass back and forth at night. This is for their safety also."

"Masks," said Felkior. "Any masks which are required I will supply. And in my office as Keeper of the Book it is proper to me to warn the citizens that there is a new mask active."

"I will speak again to the authorities," I said. "This is no longer a single incident affecting a foreigner. A citizen has been killed."

"A crippled woman of the servant classes," said Corius. "They will not care."

"The Countess is powerful," I suggested. "Can I not approach her to lend her assistance?"

"No!" they said in one voice, then glanced among themselves. At last Felkior, with his usual courtesy, explained.

"The Countess is dangerous, Bass. One does not pursue a rat by setting one's barn on fire." He drew his charcoal-grey robe close about him, as one does who feels a chill.

So there I had to leave it.

Private Journal of Sallia

Not dated

Mama has been killed I have been weeping all day the countess cuffed me and sent me away oh mama.

Private Journal of Gregorius Bass

The fourth of the second month

Today I gave Corius liberty that he might make what arrangements were needed in regard to his mother. I wished many times at the office that I had him with me, for petitioners still assail me. I am worn out and that is all I will write.

The fifth of the second month

A day of much busyness again, but I have nothing to report here. There is still no thread to seize upon to lead us to the murderer. The Captain of the Guard has made no reply to my letter, nor to a second concerning Corius's mother. None of the investigations made at Corius's instigation have produced any form of fruit. The leaders of the Calarian community besiege me daily and are not prepared to be satisfied that I have done all that can be done; it tries the patience that I had thought one of my virtues. It is an atmosphere of fear and desperation, and I worry for young Corius, bereft now of his mother in such ugly circumstances and with the burden of seeking her murderer falling so heavy upon him. Besides that he has had the shock of discovering, at the age of two and twenty, that he has known his father all his life but has not known him as his father – though I believe he looks upon both of the old men in that light, yet it is a wrench. He hardly speaks to me except to report and respond to my requests, where once he chattered as does a flock of birds.

He looks thin, and I fear he is not sleeping. I bespoke for him a sleeping draught, but he would not take it, saying that it were best if he could be woken at need in the night, and a sleeping

draught would prevent this. Condemn me if he would not sleep
across my doorsill if I asked it of him. He flings himself into
work with a will, but makes mistakes readily and is distracted;
today I corrected his addressing of a letter and he almost wept.
I apologised to him for my harshness and insisted he go out
and walk around, for when I am unhappy that is what does me
more good than any other thing. He said that it helped him
somewhat.

Our studies in the Book of Masks are at a standstill but I
continue my fencing lessons. Swords seem likelier than books
to be needed in this city at such a time, I much regret.

Looking back in my journal I see I wished that something
would happen. Proof if it were needed that I am a fool.

The sixth of the second month

Mende's funeral was this morning. I could not go, for the office
must remain open, but I gave Corius leave with a good will.
He thanked me more than such an action deserved, saying few
masters would do so. This is nonsense; what master would not
release a man to attend the funeral of his mother? Besides, he is
my valet, not my clerk, and helps me in the office more out of
goodwill than because it is any part of the job he was hired for.

I gave him the afternoon in addition, for it was clear he would
mar more than he would mend, as the saying goes. He is paler
than his linen shirt, and his eyes behind his mask are bloodshot.
I daresay that, could I see beneath that mask, dark bags would
be under his eyes. It is like working with a ghost.

Tonight I pressed the old men again to ask the Countess for
assistance, and again they would not.

"Why not?" I asked, "for she is a powerful woman, and surely
the murder of her servant touches her interests."

Tamas turned to his friend and master and looked at him,
and the blind old man, as it seemed, met his gaze and said, "It is
time, I think, to show him the play."

"Play?" I asked.

"We wrote a play together," said Felkior, as Tamas pulled out
a drawer from the desk and fumbled in the space behind. "We
have not dared, though, to mount it. Not for its lack of literary
merit, though it does have such a lack, but for fear of reprisals

from the Countess. For although she is not named therein, any clever man could find out that she is intended in it."

"Here," said Tamas, withdrawing a small packet and unfolding it to reveal a few sheets of paper, written in his neat hand. He passed it to me and we sat in silence while I read it. I reproduce it here without further comment, for I believe it speaks for itself. They swear that every word of it is true.

Roiklef and Samat: A Drama in Six Scenes

Persons:
Roiklef, a rake.
Samat, another.
A **Lady**.
Her **Maid**.

Scene I: A Street.
*Enter **Roiklef** and **Samat**. Roiklef is half-masked in his own face, Samat wears a mask the same, but full-wide.*
Roi: I tell you, Samat, she has quite engaged my fancy. I think I shall attempt her.
Sam: A mad adventure! Her father…
Roi: Indeed, her father. That is half the pleasure, my friend, for I daresay the untried chit shall give me little enough amusement. It is the challenge, not the goal, that I desire.
Sam: How purpose you to do it?
Roi: Why, by our most successful stratagem. You, with your low tastes, shall seduce her maid – a plump and ready pullet, from my observation, and quite in your line – and secure my entrance. And then, if I am not able to win her – I am much fallen off my prime.
Sam: Admirable. I will do it; point me at the maid.
Roi: I daresay you will point yourself at the maid soon enough, and not long after you have made the maid, I will have made the maid whose maid she is to be no maid no more.
Sam: Ha! Priceless! [*Claps him on the back.*
Exeunt.

Scene II: The Same

*Enter **Roiklef** and **Samat**.*

Roi: Samat, Samat, I would not tell this abroad, but I am quite captived by this Lady, this treasure, this – this paragon. Her innocence, and yet her passion; her youthfulness, and yet her strength; her cunning in keeping us from the notice of her father; this is a Lady, I swear, who will do great things in this our City.

Sam: She has done great things to you, my falcon-friend, who never ere now was brought to wrist.

Roi: Aye, true. I am so smitten that – [*Glances round*
Are we unobserved and unheard?

Sam: We are.

Roi: And will you not betray me? Ah, what do I ask! The earth will betray the sun before that you betray me. Hear then: I love this woman.

Sam: I had guessed it.

Roi: Hear further, then. I have foresworn other women for her.

Sam: For truth? That I had not guessed, though now you say it, I, who am with you constantly, know that it is true. You have not resorted to another since first you went in to her. And that is what? Two seasons?

Roi: Almost three. But hold, my friend, you yourself – have you been with any other bar her maid, since first you began that affair?

Sam: No – no, now that I think on't, no. I have not done so.

Roi: Meseems we are – [*Looks round again*

Sam (*whispering*)**:** We are Unmasked.

Roi: Indeed, and were the Temple to catch us, we would be whipped for not being unfaithful to our mistresses as we ought. But condemn me if I care a wood splinter for it.

Sam: You are at least in better case than I, for if the Temple caught me, it would whip me both for going to my mistress and for not going to another. But then, if her father caught you, he would kill you.

Roi: Though he would whip me first for a time, I think, to warm his arm up for the axe. Curse on him for a bloody-handed wretch! I tell you, Samat, I would marry her if she were any other noble's daughter. No, if she were the daughter of a beggar of the streets.

Sam: Why do you not steal her away and marry her secretly?

Roi: He would kill us all, the four of us, you, me and our lemans, and dance on the bones. Thank Sunshine he is ailing, and perhaps will die.

Sam: That old leatherhead will never die, he has not the patience for it.

Exeunt, laughing

Scene III: The Same

*Enter **Roiklef** and **Samat**. **Roiklef** is despondent.*

Sam: Roiklef, what is it? What ails you?

Roi: Aye, what ails me? You choose the exact question, my friend, for I have just seen the leech.

Sam: And are you ill?

Roi: Ill? Aye, ill, and all the world is ill by reason of the ill I have. For it is an ill ill, comrade, an ill which speaks, and for what it says I have no liking.

Sam: Why, what says it?

Roi: It says, I am such a disease as one who lives the life of Roiklaf's mask well may get, or it well may get him; so far, distressing, but not surprising. I have made it my business to study such diseases that I might avoid them, and have taken precautions hitherto. Yet to one who lives the life of Roiklaf – not the masked life, but the Unmasked – it is surprising, for this disease, from exposure-time to when it shows as it has shown in me, is rapid, it takes but a circuit of the moon.

Sam: And what?

Roi: And this: That for a year almost, I have been with no other than my Lady. That contrary to my mask, I have been faithful to her without wavering. And so it must be from her that I have got me this disease.

Sam: From her? Then – she, she is not faithful?

Roi: Almost I wish to murder you where you stand for saying it, and you my friend, and what you say, I fear, is the truth. Now do you see why all the world is ill?

Sam: Roiklef, I –

Roi: Hold. Samat, will you swear here before me that you have not betrayed me?

Sam: I? I would sooner betray my arm, my neck, my vitals. I, betray you?

Roi: Prove it then. Come with me to that same leech. Come on, prove it, or I prove you with my sword.

Sam: Roiklef, Roiklef, you rave, my friend, you rave.

Roi (*drawing his sword*)**:** Come to the leech. Come, you wretch, or lose your life this moment!

Sam: Roiklef, comrade! You are not yourself.

Roi: I am not myself, nor have I been myself these ten months. I wonder have I ever been myself. Will you come, or will you die in this gutter?

Sam: I – my friend, I will come. But it is unworthy of you, and the leech will confirm it. I have not touched your Lady.

Roi: Some wretch has touched her, and that wretch shall bleed. I swear it.

Exeunt, Samat at the point of Roiklef's sword

Scene IV: The Lady's Bower

*The **Lady** is discovered, seated. She is masked as an innocent young woman and is about 17 years old. Enter **Roiklef**.*

Lady: Roiklef, I had not expected you so early. [*She adds a token of seduction to her mask*

I have said it before – have a care of my father!

Roi: I care for your father no more than for the swine he most resembles. Nor care I for anything to-day, for I have found out a thing.

Lady: Oh? What thing?

Roi: A thing – my Lady, [*crosses to her, takes her hand*

I have seen a leech today.

Lady: I have never known you to be ill ere now.

Roi: But now I am, and all is ill until I find the reason, and then ill, ill!

Lady: Why, what is the matter?

Roi: I have a disease – one of those which pass only between lovers.

Lady: And you fear I have it, from our congress?

Roi: Lady, I know you have it, but not from *our* congress.

Lady: Why, what do you mean?

Roi: You sit here, masked as an innocent, but even when you don the token of having been seduced by me, you are Unmasked. You have been with another.

Lady: How dare you! You, the rake, attribute this disease to me, instead of to some other of your conquests!

Roi: Hear me now. I have not been with any woman else since first I came here to you.

Lady (*coldly, turning from him*)**:** Then it is you who are Unmasked, for your Character is never faithful.

Roi: Have you no more to say?

Lady: No more. Get hence.

Roi (*between his teeth*)**:** With such gladness as I am capable of in this world, I will get hence this moment.

Exit Roiklef.

Scene V: The Street

*Enter **Samat** and the **Maid,** severally. **Samat** is limping.*

Maid: Samat! What has happened to you? Or do you not speak to me now? You did not come the other night as we had compacted.

Sam: Dogs. Some one let loose dogs in the courtyard, the one we must pass through on our secret way to – I mean, the one I must pass through on my secret way to you. I barely escaped them.

Maid: Dogs! I knew nothing of this.

Sam: Dogs loosed by a bitch, I have no doubt.

Maid: What do you mean?

Sam: Your mistress.

Maid: I will not have you call her that. Because your friend has abandoned her…

Sam: Is that what she told you?

Maid: I will not listen, I will not listen. You need not brave the dogs any more – if there were dogs. More likely some bitch of yours bit you on the leg. Farewell, Samat, I hope your bites fester.

*Exit, hurrying. **Samat** stares after her, then exits in the other direction.*

Scene VI: The Same

*Enter **Samat** leading **Roiklef**, who is blind.*

Roi: A pox upon that pox-doctor! For make no mistake, Samat, it was his potions took my sight.

Sam: I fear you are right, my friend.

Roi: As for my other loss – well, little loss enough, I have foresworn women in any case, and I had enough use of it for one lifetime. I have been nineteen years old for almost nineteen years. The time, I think, has come to change masks.

Sam: Change masks? What will you do?

Roi: I have the Book of Masks by heart, and yet I do not know.

Sam: Go to the Keeper of Masks and ask him, then.

Roi: Perhaps I will, Samat. Perhaps I will. And you, what will you do?

Sam: I have another life already in the Temple, and it begins to draw me. I am sobered, Roiklef, by our experience and our losses – especially yours. Perhaps it is time to turn back to the Sun.

Roi: Were I you, I would turn rather to the Moon, for she shines in darkness. But as you wish. *[Stumbles.*

Condemn that doctor! It is as well for him that he is long gone.

Sam: As well indeed, for have you heard the news?

Roi: I hear nothing that you do not tell me, brother. You are my ears as much as you are my eyes.

Sam: He treated also the father of your – I mean, the nobleman who lately died.

Roi: Nobleman! The noblest thing he ever did was die. And do they suspect the doctor?

Sam: They do, but he has vanished without trace.

Roi: A charlatan and a poisoner. I would I had him under my hand this moment, I would take his eyes and his cod in vengeance. It was a bitter day that you happened on him in the market.

Sam: Happened on him? No, I heard of him from my former leman. We speak now when we meet in public, though we cannot meet in private – why, Roiklef, what is it? What pales your face?

Roi: My Lady's maid told you of the doctor?

Sam: Surely.

Roi: And her father also went to this mysterious doctor, and then died?

Sam: Yes.

Roi: Her father, who had, it seems, the same disease I have – the same disease I got from her?

Sam: What are you saying?

Roi: Samat, we never learned – from whom had she the disease?

Samat turns to audience, his face horrified.

End.

Private Journal of Sallia

Not dated

Mamas funeral today just the family and myser Tamas and the keeper came. The countess shouted at me when I asked for leave to go she was very angry but she let me though she will dock my pay for all day even though I was only gone two hours. It is not my fault my mama died. Corius and Juliana looks terrible they have not been sleeping nor have I. Tamas wept and wept he loved my mama I think I never knew because they could not say about it or be together. Bardo could not come he has duties he cannot leave he said he wold come tonight I hope he does he will hold me and that is what I need now. I cannot do anything right for the countess she is very roth with me and has struck me over and again.

Private Journal of Gregorius Bass

The seventh of the second month

Corius is out now walking for it is his half-day and I insisted that he take it, despite

(*Later*)

As I was writing of Corius, came a knock at the door and when I answered it was his sisters, in search of him. Sallia is a bustling, pert young miss who talks much, and little to the point, it seemed to me. Juliana, however, is a quiet and seemingly reflective girl, not beautiful, but pleasant, and the little that she said was all of it worth hearing. She looks as weary as does her brother, though not so pale.

I had them in, for I expected Corius back momentarily, and offered them somewhat to eat and drink, though they declined it. I am not so proud, nor so high in the world at the moment, that I will not sit and speak with my servant's sisters, and I confess I have not had the pleasure of women's company much or for some time. My sister's friends had no regard for me, which always grieved her, for she has much; I was too old in their eyes, too clumsy, and they fastened their fascination on younger and lighter men. So I am unused to feminine conversation as it includes me.

"Mysir Bass," began Sallia when they were seated, "tell me, what do you say of this murderer, this evil man who has taken our mother from us? For she was as much mother to me as to Juliana and your Corius, for all I was none of her flesh. Raised me from an infant, so she did, and treated me no different, never. And now we hear that Mysir Tamas is their father, which I will confess I never thought, for all he gave so many hours to tutor them, and would have tutored me had I wished it, which I did not, for I am no more a scholar than was my poor mother, may she have sunshine. Except that he taught me my letters, which is more than she knew, poor thing, and if she had we might have her yet, for Corius says that she was on her way to Mysir Tamas to have somewhat scrivened for her when... It is too horrible. Oh, my poor Mama!"

She sank her head in her hands, and her sister took the chance while her stream of talk was stopped a moment to say, "Mysir Bass, we do appreciate your efforts to find out the killer. Corius says that you most kindly stated that it was as important to you to find the killer of our mother as to find the killer of your countryman."

"Indeed," I said, "though My Lord would not thank me for the sentiment, Envoy that I am."

"Oh, and a good Envoy, I am sure, Mysir," began Sallia, who had recovered herself sufficiently to launch another flurry of words. "Corius reports you a kind master who serves his country and his countrymen with the most devoted loyalty. Loyalty is so important, as my mistress the Countess said to me only the other day. Indeed, my poor mother gave up her health in loyal service of the Countess, getting her terrible injuries when that evil assassin attacked her carriage – the Countess's carriage, I mean – and panicked the horses and they dashed it against a bridge-railing and it fell into the Lower Streets. Oh, it was awful, Mysir, and I remember it like yesterday, for all it was seven years come next Equinox and I but a girl. But the Countess herself was uninjured and we can only be glad of that, can we not, for such is loyalty, indeed."

"Indeed," I said, not sure to what I was agreeing, and caught a smile in the eyes of Juliana as she listened to the prattling of her stepsister. Two young women more unalike you could not meet, although much of a height one with the other; Juliana, too, has much Corius's colouring and heart-shaped face, so it is clear she is his twin, while Sallia has lighter eyes and hair (though still brown, as with all but a few Bonvidaeoans) and a round face. Also, where Juliana is very slender, Sallia is a little plump. But the physical differences are far outweighted by the differences in character.

Sallia's chatter continued, but I paid it little mind as it seemed that she required no answers of me, no more than a millstream which carries out of its mouth whatever flows into its head. To fall into it was to be carried away from any point which there might have been to the conversation, so I waited for a moment when she needed to catch breath and directed a question to Juliana – in a firm voice so as not to be overspoken.

"Mistress Juliana, may I ask if you have spoken with your brother in recent days?"

"I have, Mysir."

"Then you will have seen his condition – that he lacks sleep, that he loses weight who is already a slender youth, that he twitches and starts if one drops some item – as sometimes I do, for I am not dextrous – " Realizing that I was beginning to sound like Sallia, I reigned myself in. "Mistress, what is there to do for him? He is a good fellow, the best servant I have had, and I would count him, indeed, as a friend and comrade, for his father and yours is a gentleman and his circumstances are none of his making. With a different cast of fate I could be his servant, and would make a poorer one withal. I have a great affection

for him, truth be told, and to see him hollow-eyed and pale as a
girl grieves me. Yet he has the pride of his excellence, and will
not be told to care for himself."

She was silent so long that, had she not held up a hand to
still her, Sallia had drowned us in another monologue. Then she
looked me in the eye, and hers, I fancied, was a small matter
moist behind her mask.

"Mysir, your concern for your servant does you much credit,
and truly you are the Gentle Knight." (For I have taken to wearing that mask as my main one, unless I am being the Envoy or
unless I am in commerce with such masks as may endanger me
through my ignorance. This is not a time or a place for an Innocent Man.)

"I will speak to him," she said. "He will heed me, for I am
closer to him than a sister usually is, by reason of our being born
together. You need not fear for the welfare of your good servant.
Have you a sleeping draught by?"

I said I had.

"I will speak to him and he will take it. His knowledge of
your concern, I think, will help him to thrive also. I can only
urge his grief as a reason that he has not so far remarked it, for
truly, none of us have noticed much that goes forward in the last
few days."

"I understand entirely," I said, "there is nothing to excuse."

At that juncture rang out a bell from the nearby square to tell
that it was almost sunset.

"But, my good young women," I said, "it grows late, and
Corius has not come. Little as I wish to quit me of your company, I am anxious that you not travel under night, for as we
know, the night city is not safe. Do you wish my escort to your
homes?"

"Mysir, we could not ask it of you," said Juliana, and Sallia
much the same in many more words. "My friend Bardo," she
said finally, "has men who look to him, and one waits outside to
escort us. But what you say is true, Mysir, we should be going, it
is not safe to travel even escorted in some quarters after my Lord
Sun is absent, for the people who owe allegiance to the night are
not such that we should encounter them, and..."

Juliana, at this juncture, rose, and raised her sister by the
arm and let her, still clacking, to the door, where by some effort

she had Sallia make her farewells. They blessed me once again for my solicitude for Corius and departed, Juliana looking back once to smile, at which I smiled in return.

They were not long away – not longer than was required for me to brew myself a drink for my refreshment – when Corius at last returned, saying that he had encountered them not far from our dwelling. "And I am under instructions," he said, "to take your sleeping draught tonight, and to eat more and take better care of myself, under your guidance and guardianship." He seemed rueful but amused, and I sensed an affection for his sister and, I think, for me.

Private journal of Sallia

Not dated

Today I went with Juliana and met Bass Coriuses master he is a big man and speaks very formal. He was kind about our mother like Corius said and he was worried about Corius not sleeping and we said we would tell him to take care of himself. He wanted to escort us home. I do not think he is clever though. I told him all about the countess and I do not think he listened to a word he just sat and looked at us. Juliana likes him I think.

The Countess is in a good temper today and calm I have not seen her so calm in a long time she greeted me when I came in from my half-day and smiled at me she was going out herself just then. It just goes to show she is a good mistress really and worthy of my loyalty whatever Corius thinks. She is angry sometimes but she is a great lady and I am just her maid after all although – but I will not write of that it is not something to put in my journal or speak about to any one.

The weather is very cold and damp and foggy it is the kind of weather when my poor mama would have pain in her old injury I think of her all the time and keep meaning to speak to her of some what but then I remember she is gone.

Private Journal of Gregorius Bass

The eighth of the second month

Last night a third murder, and at last the Guard take notice, for it
was a lesser member of the Commissioners of Masks, the body
which, to hear Corius tell it, governs the City, rather than the
King or his Council. It is said that Captain Portavin has lost his
place, and is lucky not to have lost his liberty and entered his
own dungeons for his inaction on the matter. (He has himself
connections in the Commissioners, else would he have suffered
this worse fate.) The whole City resembles most closely an ant
heap turned over with a shovel. I have, belatedly, been inter-
viewed by a Sergeant of the Guard, who brought a clerk to take
his notes and said to him constantly, "Write that down," as if the
man were not doing so. He breathed heavily through his mouth
and sweated, a corpulent man without imagination. I should
not speak so ill of him but I am grieved that the Guard takes
such notice of persons and their station instead of serving all
impartially as they ought.

I can at least now tell the Calarians that the Guard is investigating. Not that this reassures me, but it will reassure them.

The ninth of the second month

Corius is somewhat better and able to help me more in the office
today. This is as well, for petitioners still come, and we must tell
them the story over and again. I sent him also to the harbour
to any Calarian shipping which might be in, for I expected today a reply from My Lord if he was prompt in answering to my
request for his support in convincing the Bonvidaeoans to take
action in search of the murderer. That situation has now – in the
saddest way – taken care of itself, but it would still be comforting to tell the Calarians here that my superior has offered them
his influence. There was no message today, however, so I will
send him again tomorrow when another ship is due.

The tenth of the second month

I received today the expected letter sealed from My Lord. I will try not to speak to my petitioners of its contents, but fear I cannot dissemble very well. I am an honest man and this is not a city for honest men.

Official reply from Darion, Lord Rivers, Undersecretary to the Foreign Minister of Calaria, to Gregorius Bass, Envoy of Calaria in the city of Bonvidaeo

The seventh of the second month

Mysir Bass,

In regard to the matter of which you inform us as touching the unfortunate death of a Calarian fuller in the city of Bonvidaeo.

I regret to state that we are unable to release additional funds to you for the resolution of this matter.

It appears from your dispatch that this is an isolated incident and unlikely to be repeated. Your usual resources should therefore be adequate to its resolution.

Trusting that this is well understood,
Rivers
(per A. Tailor.)

Private journal of Gregorius Bass

The eleventh of the second month

A butcher was shot by the Guard early this morning while going home late from his lawful business.

A new appointment has been made to the Commissioners of Masks. Corius says he is one of the Countess's "pets". I forebore to inquire further into his meaning.

"And in the morning," he said, "we must speak of an ill thought I have. But it can wait until then." It is late, and he is more tired even than I.

The twelfth of the second month

I left Corius asleep this morning and went to the office alone. We are less besieged now than formerly, for the word has gone around among the Calarian expatriates that the Watch are at last investigating, and I have resumed my study of the Book of Masks. He has taught me sufficient that I am able to read parts of it for myself and interpret the contents, with some difficulty, so I have been seeking to discover the meaning of the mask worn by Juliana – simply as an exercise for my own understanding. It was not as the maid's mask worn by Sallia, a black domino with a pattern of white lace, but a dark grey mask covering the whole upper face. Up the sides, cross-stitches of green, gold and white, and a single silver sequin above each eye. So far I have not found it.

Corius appeared at noon, half asleep, and attempted to berate me for allowing him to sleep; I, in turn, attempted to send him home. We achieved at length a truce and I reminded him of his words the previous night of some ill thought which had come to him. He sobered.

"Let me show you something." He rustled in a drawer and found a map of the city. "This is out of date but for present purposes that is not important. Mysir, would you mark upon it the locations of the three murders?"

I looked at him in puzzlement, but took up pen and ink and marked, as best I could calculate, the location of the first murder at the back of the mercer's shop, then the location of his mother's death (I had been shown it), and last, the place of decease of the unfortunate councilman. He corrected the last – I had moved it over by a street – and said, "Now connect the three, if you would be so good."

I drew a triangle with my marks at the points, and looked at him again.

"What is inside the triangle?"

I looked down at the paper. In almost the centre of the triangle was a house marked as "Coslian Manor". I still saw no significance, and said so.

"My apologies, Mysir, I had forgotten, you are a stranger to our city. The old Coslian Manor, as it is marked upon this map, is now the town residence of the Countess."

"What is it that you are saying, Corius? What is your ill thought? That the Countess has aught to do with these crimes?"

"Nay, for she has means enough without that. My ill thought is that some other person connected with the Countess's household is responsible for them. And Mysir – my suspicion has fallen upon Bardo."

"Bardo! But he is the very man –"

"Aye, Mysir, the very man who is the conduit for the investigation. The very man who knows everything we are doing. The very man who is guarding my sisters. The very man."

"But Corius – what grounds have you for your suspicions? A triangle upon a map?"

"More than that, Mysir, though that was what began my thought. Bardo is secretive. That is to be expected – he is a leader, perhaps a high leader from what I understand, in – let us say a secretive organization and leave it at that. But things he has said – he seems, at times, to be keeping more secrets than one. He masks as a Porter, but his hands are smoother than yours, which hold a pen, at least. Were I he, I would wear gloves. He is an aristocrat, Mysir, and I do not trust aristocrats. I believe he has his own interests, and that they do not necessarily include discovering the killer. In fact, they may very well include *not* discovering the killer. They may include *being* the killer."

I was silent for some time, attempting to comprehend all that he had told me. At last, I said, "But, Corius – you have no way to test these beliefs, to show them true or mistaken. And you are building speculation upon speculation. It is – a tall structure on a narrow foundation, I suggest to you."

"True," he said, something downcast. "True, Mysir. But what if I should prove it true? What if I should gain the evidence?"

"Then we would be facing a powerful aristocrat with backing from the underground, who is also an insane killer without a shred of mercy."

"Aye, Mysir. But if we were facing such a one, would it not be better to know?"

I could not deny this. "How, though, can we find out? Can Sallia tell us anything?"

"Nay, for the man is not a fool, and he tells Sallia nothing that he does not wish generally known. But if I can follow him, eavesdrop, hear what he says to his followers..."

"Corius, no! He will kill you!"

"Only if he catches me."

"But surely he will catch you. He must have security, he must have ways to prevent his movements and his plans from being spied upon, or he would not still be alive."

He was downcast. "True, Mysir, true. But there must be a way. There must be some way to penetrate that security and find out his true plans."

At that moment came in a Calarian to consult me and we said no more of the matter. I sent Corius home early and came back to discover him pacing the room and muttering. I ensured that he had eaten well, once again made him take a sleeping draught and sent him off to bed. Apart from his need for sleep, I do not want him wandering the night in some foolish attempt to discover Bardo's plans.

The thirteenth of the second month

It was as well that Corius did not wander the night last night, for the Butcher has claimed another victim. A minor nobleman, this time, who was walking the High Paths – or staggering them, rather, for it appears he was very drunk. It is somewhat comforting to think that he may consequently not have suffered, or been aware of the assault. He was found this morning spreadeagled upon a roof not far distant from the mansion of the Countess. He was in the usual condition of such victims. By various marks it appeared that he had been struck unconscious, or dead, upon the High Path, dragged thence to the roof and there eviscerated and arranged in the manner – well, in that manner which I have previously mentioned. At night the spot was not visible, but in the daylight it could be seen from another of the High Paths by reason of his colourful clothing and the quantities of blood involved.

All this we have from Bardo in person, for he reported to us at the office, in his guise as a porter, delivering paper and other such supplies. He is a strong young man, closer to Corius's age than mine, not tall, but broad-shouldered; the guise of a porter befits him well. I had not previously met him and was impressed by his air of confidence and competence, although, like Corius, I do not entirely trust him. It is somewhat suspicious that he knows so much so soon, however good his informers. And his hands, indeed, betray him as one of the upper classes – as one, therefore, who is permitted to traverse the High Paths.

Corius had out tonight the old men's books and charts of genealogy and was attempting to trace out who would benefit from the death of the young noble last night. He reached no conclusion, as Tamas thought he would not, for madmen kill opportunely rather than to advance some rational cause. Corius is not so sure, believing that this particular madman has also a scheme in mind.

"Of course," he said, "it may well be that this latest killing was not for who he was but for what he knew, or had done, or had said. After all, no one benefited by inheritance from any of the other deaths. It is just that he is a nobleman, and breeding and inheritance are such preoccupations of the nobility that it is the first place I thought to look. Besides, I am out of the networks of gossip since my absence from the city, so these books must speak to me instead. I should go and see Sallia. Half her value to the Countess is that she gossips with the other maids."

"Then you must go to see her tomorrow," I said, "during my fencing lesson, for you need not attend upon me at that time. I must admit, I have some concern for her welfare because of her proximity to Bardo, for all you believe his affection for her to be genuine. Ascertain for us that she is as well as might be, has all she needs and is safe, or as safe as one can reasonably be in this thrice-condemned city."

"Thank you, Mysir," he said, "you are kind to have concern for her, and right to do so, also; I myself have been wondering how she does. Tomorrow I will go."

The fourteenth of the second month

Today to the old men's house after closing the office. Corius went off to see Sallia, and returned looking stunned, for Bardo had been there, and, unlooked-for, had confided something of his plans to Corius, out of Sallia's hearing.

"Felkior", he said, "Tamas – Mysir Bass. I need your advice."

We indicated our pleasure was to give it.

"I have – word of a plot. A plot to rock the foundations of the City!" He leaned forward and gestured its magnitude. "A plot insane, yet with every chance of horrible success, which could make the gutters run with blood and bring us all to ruination."

"And you want our advice on how to stop it?" I asked.

"Nay, Master, a step further back. I want advice on *whether* to stop it. For it is a plot to kill an evil man."

"An evil man whose death would bring blood and destruction? A politician?" Tamas asked.

"Nay, a priest. The Archpriest of the Sun."

They were silent, shocked. Then the Keeper of the Book, with his scholarly courtesy, turned to me and explicated.

"The Archpriest of the Sun," he said, "is the highest prelate in the city, by virtue of the Sun's supremacy in the heavenly pantheon. Accordingly, he is the Voice of the Gods to King and Council, a man of great influence and significance. He annually, at the Winter Solstice, embodies the Sun in His re-emergence to life and power. And this will take place tomorrow ten days."

"And is this plot," he asked Corius, "to kill him prior to the ceremony?"

"Nay," said he, "during."

"During the ceremony? During? While he embodies the Lord Sun Himself? Madness!"

"Madness, aye, so said I. But well-laid madness. I think they could achieve it – and then, where are we?"

"Hunted down," said Tamas softly. "Hunted down, tied up, and whipped into strips."

"Exactly," said Corius.

I must have looked confused, for he explained. "Master, only the Personalist faction, those who do not accept the Characterist view that 'the mask is the man', could be responsible for such a plot, for Personalists would see a man wearing the mask of the Sun, rather than the embodiment of the Sun in a man. The least religious Characterist that ever twitched alive would sooner fire a crossbow into his own eye than at the Sun Embodied. It would be without point, for you cannot kill the Sun. But you can kill a man. And if they shoot him, and he dies, then it is proof that he is a man and not the Sun."

"It is nothing of the kind," said Tamas, "and if they think that it will be seen to prove Personalism true they are great fools. But it will be seen to prove Personalism dangerous and pernicious, and as you, who are a better thinker, have perceived, the Archpriest's death will then be the first of many. Personalism is illegal, true. But many things are illegal which, if they make no great harm, are winked at. It is only our harmlessness that is our shield, and our mask and cloak."

"You are a Personalist?" I asked, far behind events.

"I? Yes, I am a Personalist. What do you think I argue about so much with my good friend the Keeper?"

"Then you are a Characterist, Sir?"

"I am. And my friend is too modest. He is not merely a Personalist. He is almost *the* Personalist, the leader of their movement."

"Tchah," said Tamas with a gesture. "Hardly. A leader, at most, of the moderate and pious faction. Not of any rabble who would assassinate Archpriests – though that will not protect me. The City Guard are not famous for making subtle distinctions."

"But if – but how – but why – " I asked, gesturing between the two.

"He is my friend," explained the good old man, knowing what I was trying to ask without having to see the gestures. And when he said it, it was enough of an explanation.

"So what of this plot? They have kept it carefully enough from me, I need not tell you," said Tamas to Corius after some silence.

"Crossbows," he summarised. "Not one, but many, hidden under cloaks. One might miss, or one man be captured. They will pack the crowd, fill the upper windows. If the Guard come across one they will not think to look for others."

"And when? At the high point of the ceremony, the dawn moment?" Tamas guessed.

"Aye," said Corius, "then."

"We must stop it," I said.

"You are right," said Corius. "Little as I would grieve the Archpriest, the consequences for our people are not to be thought of."

"Have not been thought of, by the plotters – or they do not care," muttered Tamas.

"But whether or not you would grieve for the Archpriest does not enter in," I said. "He is a man, is he not? Then it is murder, and we must stop it."

Tamas sat up as if stricken.

"Sad the day," he cried. "I am chastened by the Innocent Man. Yes, Mysir, yes! You speak the truth of innocence. Murder is an evil, and we must not give our faces to it, be the victim who it might. He is, as you so rightly say, a man. In fact, he is my brother."

"Oh, come, Father," said Corius. "That goes beyond."

"He is not metaphorical," said the Keeper.

"No," again Tamas. "No, he is my brother of the womb. We were twins."

Corius was silent for several seconds, then: "The *Archpriest* is my *uncle*?"

"Well – yes, that would follow," Felkior said wryly.

Corius was silent, then, in a low, angry tone, as if choked, he asked, "Are there perhaps any other relatives you would like to mention to me? The Countess, perhaps? King Emilion?"

Tamas looked down, shamed. "Corius, I apologise. We should not have hidden it from you. When you were young, my youth and its indiscretions were to be put behind me, not spoken of. And later, when I gained some distance, when I could take pride in something, at least, that came out of those years, even if un-intended – I never brought myself to speak of it, somehow. The time never seemed right to give you such a shock. And so, in fact, the time at which I had to give it to you was *not* the right time. I was wrong, and I ask your forgiveness."

Corius still seemed incapable of speech, but at length he crossed the space between him and the good man his father and embraced him silently. At length, Tamas spoke again.

"And to answer your question," he said, "I know of no other living member of my family or Mende's. We had an elder brother, who inherited from our father, but he died in a foolish acci-dent and the estate – such as it still was – went back to the Crown, for Benor and I had been given to the Temple and were legally barred from inheriting. Later, when I lost my priesthood, I was attainted in blood from any claim upon the estate or titles. You have no more inheritance from your father than from your mother, lad. I am sorry."

"I am not," said Corius through welling tears, "though it would be useful in its way, I suppose. I do not admire the aristocracy so much that I wish to be admitted to it, but some money would always be welcome."

"Little enough of that was left even in my brother's day. It was the title and little more that he inherited, and he spent most of what there was. Would have spent the title if he could. I cannot condemn him – I was no better, indeed worse, for he broke no vows."

"Your regret does you great credit," broke in the rich voice of Felkior, "but it is time to set it in the past and bethink ourselves of our plans for the future. How shall we prevent this assassination?"

"We must convince Bardo to abandon his plot," said I. "Clearly, he does not realize the chaos it would cause."

"I think he does," replied Corius. "When he told me, I tried to convince him as you say – argued all that we have said here, with the exception of the worth of – Uncle Benor's human life, which I must say did not occur to me and would have carried little weight with him in any case. It seems he is determined to proceed in spite of the tragedy it would bring down on Personalists throughout the city."

"Can we hide the Personalists?" I asked.

"We can," said Tamas, "for though many Moonpriests are also Characterists – orthodox in that much – they would take the risk of hiding other dissidents for my sake. I hesitate to ask it, though, for two reasons."

"Please tell me them."

"Firstly, that the authorities will be suspicious if all known Personalists disappear suddenly just before the solstice. We are watched, lightly and by fools, it is true, but not so lightly nor by such fools that they would miss our mass disappearance at such a time. And that, in turn, would be likely to cause the plot to be discovered and bring down Bardo's faction's vengeance on us who are more moderate. That vengeance would be likely to take the form of betraying our locations. Still there would be bloodshed, and now the Moonpriests would be implicated and purged as well and I would have betrayed both of my allegiances – which is my second reason. I fear to bring the notice of the authorities on the people of the Moon."

"Then if we cannot convince Bardo to cease his plot, nor hide those who will be its innocent victims, can we foil it in some other way – make it impossible to carry out?"

"The only way I can think of to do that," said Corius, "is to betray Bardo himself and his plot to the authorities. Not only will they probably find out that it was I who did so, and take revenge, but that would destroy Sallia – her mother, her lover and her brother all killed in so short a time – even if she did not get caught up in the purge herself. My sister is dear to me, for all her faults, and I will not risk her so. Nor am I avid to die myself, if it comes to it."

We argued and proposed and counter-argued for an hour, but our conclusions were two only: That we must prevent the success of the plot in some way that did not require the coop-eration of either Bardo or the authorities, and did not place the Personalists at just as much risk as they already faced; and that we could not by any means think of a way to do so.

Corius was morose as we walked home in the gathering dark, and to cheer him I sought other topics. "Your sister," I said at random, "Juliana – tell me more of her, for I much enjoyed her company that recent evening."

"Did you so?" he asked.

"Yes, she is a young woman of understanding, as it seems to me," I said. "Good Tamas educated her also, I gathered from Sallia?"

"He did, though it is not common to educate women in this city."

"Nor in my country," I replied, "for women who are educated – well, it is not something that a respectable woman would do."

"It is much the same here – respectable women of the upper and merchant classes are kept ignorant, for ignorance and inno-cence are often confused. But Juliana is a woman of no social consequence and so may be educated without scandal, for no-body would trouble to pay attention to the fact – and it is a piece of our father's rebellion, for he must rebel against everything."

He did not seem to be implying that she *was* a courtesan, but I asked delicately nevertheless. "So – I could not make out her profession, though you have taught me to read the masks somewhat."

He laughed, a little bitterly. "She is not a courtesan, if that is your thought, for she is somewhat deficient in beauty for that profession."

I protested that I had not thought it, but did not correct his estimation of his sister. Truly, she is plainer than some women, but has somewhat about her which makes this of little consequence.

"Nay, she is a costumier, a significant profession in this city, and one that requires a knowledge of the Book of Masks – which she had of Tamas – as well as a knowledge of the arts of cloth and adornment, which she had of our mother. And so she is in an honest trade to which she is well suited. She is well known, too, to our friends the mercers, for she gives them custom. She was acquainted, in fact, with the first victim of the Butcher. And also, as it happens, with the third, for he had been a customer at one time."

"Remarkable, that she should know three of the four," I said idly, then frowned. This accursed city had made me too suspicious, for I said slowly, "I do not suppose that she could be involved..."

"Nay," he said, almost too quickly. "I know that for a fact. She is not, could not be involved. In fact, I know for certain where she was at the time of each of the deaths."

"Only a remarkable coincidence, then," I said.

"Only that," he said, and fell silent.

We did not speak further until we had come to the house, and then only of such matters as our meal.

Private Journal of Sallia

Not dated

Corius came today to ask if I was all right I said I was doing as well as might be. He said his master myser Bass was concerned for me that was kind. He asked too if I knew ought about the nobelman killed last night. I said no I heard nothing except he was a fool and had lots of women. He said that is like every nobleman he ever heard of. He spoke to Bardo after and they thought I did not hear. Bardo thinks I do not know about his plans against the archpreist but I do. The archpreist is a bad man I do not like him so really it is all right what Bardo plans. Corius got scared when he heard you could tell by his voice. He tried to tell Bardo no but Bardo does not like to hear no that is why I never say it to him I just say what he wants and then make him change his mind another way you can always move mens minds more easily after you have given them their pleasure so says the countess and she is right as always. She should know after all. I did not say to Corius that the nobelman was one of the countesses lovers I did not think that was important she has so many I had almost forgotten it besides I think she has set him aside now. Before he was killed I mean.

Private Journal of Gregorius Bass

The fifteenth of the second month

Again for fencing after closing up the office. My muscles grow accustomed to the exercise and do not pain me as they did; also, I begin to be faster, having learned the forms well enough that I need not think in order to perform them.

Tamas suggested tonight that he should speak to Bardo, and Corius went to arrange it and returned saying that Bardo was willing. He has not told Bardo that he has confided in us, for Bardo required his word that he would tell nobody. This troubled me, for I had taken Corius for a man of his word.

"I am not a nobleman," he replied, "despite my paternal descent, and honour is less to me than the lives of my family and friends. Could I keep my word and not endanger them, I would do so, and you need have no fear of dishonesty from me when lives are not threatened. But I will not let a quibble of a knightly code of which I have not the benefit prevent me from an action in defense of my own."

Felkior laughed. "In this city," he observed, "your Corius has the right of it, for it is proper to a Servant to think and act in such a way. If Bardo does not remember that, perhaps he is a nobleman, as we have suspected before. But Corius, it is also proper to a Servant to conceal such matters from his master – what say you?"

"I say that my master is not only my master but also my companion and a comrade-in-arms in these threatening times – if I may so call you, master. And from my comrade-in-arms I will not conceal what I judge he needs to know."

"Though you are a rogue, you are a right-hearted rogue, it seems me," I replied. "And although the idea of one morality for the high-born and another for the low disturbs me, it seems that it is universally practiced nonetheless, whether I wish it or wish it not. And so I must be content, and glad to call you comrade-in-arms, for I had rather your true loyalty than your false word."

"Well said, Sir Gentle Knight, and my hand on it," said Corius, and clasped my hand firmly in his slender fingers.

The sixteenth of the second month

Tamas offers good news. He has spoken to Bardo, at Corius's instance, and by many arguments has convinced him to abandon his intent.

"I let him explain what Corius had already told us, falling in with his stratagem," he said, "then told him, first, that he would gain nothing for our people; and second, that he would lose much; and third, that the guard are not quite such fools as he takes them for, at which he smiled. But he appeared most moved at my argument that the Characterists would lose the point he wished to make, and focus only on the violence by Personalists as a focus for their despite, and pursue us to our deaths to no good purpose. I suggested that if he must attack the Archpriest he should do so in some way which was humiliating, but not fatal, such as with aged eggs or overripe fruit – but not at a moment when he personated the Sun, lest the pious Characterists see only blasphemy and the pretend-pious a cause for persecution. Rather, he should choose the moment before the mask was on him, and remove his dignity."

"Did you mention your relationship?" I asked.

"I did not, for he might take it that I wanted to preserve my brother's life simply because he is my brother. There is little enough love between us, and I would not regret to see him humbled – if it had been done during his priestly training he would be a better man today, though probably some other would have been Archpriest. I do not wish his death, though, or any other man's if it comes to it. If only we could have our freedom without deaths!"

"Blood is the coin of freedom, so they say," said Corius darkly.

"Blood is the coin of power, and without power we cannot free ourselves, and no one else will free us," the old man replied bitterly.

We were silent for a little, then Felkior said, "And did Bardo give his word?"

Tamas cast up his eyes, remembering. "He thanked me for my counsel, and commended my wisdom and concern for our people, and said, 'It is true, violence such as I proposed can only inflame matters in the City, to no gain for our cause. Your suggestion is an excellent one and I will convey to my people orders changed accordingly. Thank you, Mysir Tamas, for your visit, and please thank Corius for bringing us in contact; I believe he is your son, recently acknowledged? He does you credit, a man of intelligence and discretion.'"

"Were those his words exact?" asked Corius. "'I will convey to my people orders changed accordingly'?"

"His words exact – I have been a secretary many years, and it has honed my memory for the spoken word."

"It sounds to me like a promise," I said.

"Aye, Mysir," said Corius, "but – forgive me – you are at times the Innocent Man."

We are all grown too suspicious. Where is trust in such a time, in such a place?

Private Journal of Sallia

Not dated

Myser Tamas came to see Bardo and wanted him not to kill the archpreist. Bardo said he would not but not really. Corius does not want him to do it I wonder why because Corius does not like the temple or the preists either and nor does myser Tamas. I think he said it would make the authorities angry with the personalists well the authorities already are angry with the personalists that is why they are criminals. I wonder if Corius told myser Tamas even though he promised not to. Corius does not always keep his promises not like Bardo if he is going to do something different he just never promises like he has never promised to marry me even though I want him to and I think he wants it too sometimes it is because of who he is he cannot do it. He thinks I do not know who he is well he is wrong but I will not say anything to let him know I know. People think I always say everything I think and I do but some of it I say only to my journal and nobody else knows that is why I hide it like I do and some of it I just say to myself in my head. Bardo was very nice to me tonight I wonder if he would be if he knew who I am or if he knew I know who he is.

Private Journal of Gregorius Bass

The seventeenth of the second month

[No entry.]

The eighteenth of the second month

The Butcher last night claimed his fifth victim, one of the Watch this time. This one has broken Corius's pattern, for it was at some distance from the house of the Countess. However, it has suggested a new pattern to him. In almost every case, there have been four nights between the killings – except for the first and second (the Calarian and Mende), where there were only two nights. The next killing, therefore, he believes will be upon the eve of Solstice. He will speak of this, he says (although not of his other theory) to Bardo, that his people might be particularly alert that night.

We discussed this theory of patterns at the house of the old men. "In the victims, however", I said, "there is no pattern in particular. A foreign merchant; a servant woman; a member of the Commissioners of Masks; a minor noble; and now, a watch-man."

"Ah," Corius argued, "this very lack of pattern is a pattern. The murderer is killing one of every group in the City, and so all are equally terrified."

"You know who is missing," said his father.

"Aye. The priests," he replied.

"I would not go garbed as a priest the night before Solstice if I were you, gentlemen," said Tamas. I think he takes Corius's theory seriously.

The nineteenth of the second month

The new Watch Captain is threatened with dismissal, for he has made no more progress than Portavin and now one of his own has been murdered by the lunatic. The investigation is in disarray, according to Bardo, who came to see us today and appears to have sources of information within the Watch. Corius is still suspicious of him but managed, I think, not to show it; I am not as suspicious, but was probably not so successful at concealing it, for I dissemble poorly.

"And your own investigation? Do you make any progress?" I asked.

"Sadly, little enough," he said. "We had thought that some one of the Countess's might be involved, since all of the killings before now had been in proximity to her house. But perhaps not – although the Countess herself, with several of her people, was in the general vicinity of this latest killing, attending a party. We are checking now upon any connections between those people and all of the victims."

"What of the Countess herself?" asked Corius. "She is ruthless enough."

"Ruthless, but quite sane, I think," said Bardo. "Besides, she has a roomful of witnesses who can swear to her whereabouts."

At this moment we were interrupted by a Calarian wishing a permit, and he fell back into character as a porter and I dismissed him with a gratuity. He smiled wryly at me behind the petitioner's back and pocketed it, then left whistling tunelessly.

The twentieth of the second month

This morning Corius's bed had not been slept in. When I took him to task he at first would not say where he had been, attempting to imply a leman, but I am not so much the Innocent Man as that. Asked outright to deny that he had been spying on Bardo, he confessed that this was the case. "I have found," he said, "a house not far from the Temple where there is activity I do not understand. I know the low-street which leads to it; tonight I plan to strap myself beneath the bridge which carries the main street above it, and investigate more closely the traffic thereto."

"And if I forbade it?"

"Do not forbid it, master, for I do not wish to leave your service," he said in a tone which was almost pleading. Although I had grave misgivings for him, I had not the heart to deny him, and it seemed that it would do little good to do so. I insisted, however, that he go home and sleep, leaving the little business of the office to me for the day. It was as well that there were few to consult me, for I was distracted with concern for the youth.

Returning at night, I woke him – with some misgivings – and as we ate, attempted to convince him to allow me to come also, to be nearby should he require the assistance of my blade. He refused, but did offer me a role, which I have just returned from performing.

"I saw", he said, "from a distance, a delivery made, and marked the carter, a man of notable ugliness with a squint and a wen. This morning after you sent me off I went in another guise to ask if I could hire his services for tonight, and he said he had a task already but his friend could help me if I wished. I visited the friend, in case he asked, but," he grinned, "we were unable to reach an accommodation on price, and I will get my carting needs met elsewhere. I suspect that there will be another delivery tonight.

"You can assist me by hiring a carriage under which I can cling, and driving across the bridge. I will fling a small stone at the horse's leg, and it will kick and falter. You, then, will stop to see to the horse at the crest of the bridge, in such a spot that the shadow of the carriage hides me as I slip over the parapet – if you can stop the carriage so that the rear wheel is almost beside the parapet, the front wheel out a little, and get down on the parapet side and stand where you will hide me, so much the better. I will swing under, and strap myself beneath – I have done it before, on this very bridge – and none shall remark me, clothed in black in the darkness and with a full mask. Then when the carter passes under, I shall see his delivery and perhaps hear somewhat to my advantage."

"It is a daring scheme," I declared, "and I see you are not to be dissuaded, so I will help you, with thanks that you trust me in its execution. But can I not take up a position nearby after you have hidden, to come to your aid if needed?"

"Nay, Mysir, for I fear you and I may be watched, and to lurk in the vicinity would bring suspicion. I am better served by secrecy. Go you on to the house of the old men; the weather tonight will be adequate explanation for the carriage."

"And how shall you return from beneath the bridge?" I asked. "For if secrecy and lack of suspicion is your goal, I can hardly have the horse stumble again on the same bridge returning."

"What you say is true," he said. "There is a ridge in the low street, however, beneath the bridge, and the cart will bump over it when it returns from the delivery. When it does so I can drop into the cartbed unheard, and in the darkness unremarked. I will leave the cart at the next opportunity, where there are shadows and means to climb, and then I will make my way, in turn, to the house of my father and the Keeper."

It sounded like a plan of considerable risk, and I said so, but he was adamant, and I soon saw that he could not be convinced; "for," he said, "if I am right and Bardo goes ahead with his original plan, the risk is far more certain for me and mine."

I carried out the first part of his scheme, and sit now with the old men, waiting for his reappearance.

The twenty-first of the second month

Corius returned unharmed last night, but I had not leisure to update my entry, for there was much for us to talk of. The cases handed in at the door of the house were such as might hold crossbows – certainly not eggs, from the behavior of one of the men who dropped one. Nor did the cartbed smell of eggs and aged fruit, but of the oil used upon weapons.

Bardo, it seems, is proceeding with his original plan.

"There was another thing which disturbed me," said Corius.

"What was that?" his father asked.

"When I was leaving the Back Ways, a pair of denizens bracketed me."

"That certainly disturbs *me*," said Tamas.

"Hush, Father. I gave them Sign but they laughed and dragged me to see their overlord. Apparently I had strayed into a gang's purlieu. That part did not formerly belong to any gang, it was Open Way."

"Much has changed in the year you were abroad," Tamas remarked.

"The overlord's lair was an ill-lit and ill-smelling cellar – among worse scents I think I detected rotting food and sour beer – and he was an ill-smelling rogue who was, from what I could see, best looked at in a poor light. He scowled at me from behind his desk of a board over two barrels, while the left-hand bravo wheezed next to my ear and the right-hand one clamped my arm so hard in his rough hand that I began to lose the feeling of it. The overlord leaned forward and breathed dung-breath at me, and then said, 'There is a charge to pass the Way of Gulls.'

"I will admit that I was panicked, between the reek and the pain in my arm and the real danger of the situation. All I could think of was that I had rather been captured by Bardo, who, if ruthless, can at least be talked to; and so vivid was the thought that I muttered his name under my breath.

"The overlord pulled back – which was to the good – and closed one eye the better to see me. I think his left was weak.

"'What's that, lad?'" (Corius's imitation was of a gruff, rasping but somewhat startled voice.)

"'Is there a charge to Bardo's leman's brother?' I said, as bravely as I might.

"He cast a glare at the two bravos, and the right-hand one let me go suddenly. As the feeling rushed into my arms I was hard-put not to cry out. The left one was slower to comprehend, but let me go and backed off too. They sheathed their knives.

"'Have you a token?' asked the overlord.

"Of course I had none. I drew myself up and bluffed. 'Not on a mission such as tonight's, you fool,' I hissed at him, and looked around as if for lurking agents of the Watch. 'What if I were to be captured?'"

"He nodded. 'Your name?' he said suddenly.

"'Corius,' I said, 'and my sister, Bardo's leman, is Sallia. You must know of Sallia.'

"They all three agreed, nodding, aye, they had heard of Sallia, of course.

"'Well then,' I said, and the overlord, still scowling, told the right-hand one, the shorter, to show me the nearest ladder up to the middle streets."

"My dear Corius," I said, perturbed, "I told you not to go."

"Indeed you did, Master," he said, "but it was necessary. And now besides what else I found out, we know this: That Bardo's is a name to conjure with among the Rats."

I looked at him, puzzled.

"Master, the Rats are what those who live in the Low Ways call themselves," he said patiently.

"You think he has bought them?" asked Felkior.

"No, I think he has cowed them," replied my servant. "And that worries me far more; for it is a token of how formidable he has become."

We talked around and around, unable to escape our two options: Betray Bardo and risk what we sought to avert, or arouse equal suspicion by causing the moderate Personalists to vanish all at once. At this point I revealed that I had taken some action myself towards this second solution, in case Corius's suspicions of Bardo proved to have foundation. I had spoken with a Calarian captain, the same who was our transport to the City, and made certain arrangements. He would be in port at the solstice, and his ship was capacious enough to hold perhaps two hundred persons if they packed in tightly. If any Uncast persons should appear – or, as far as Bonvidaeo was concerned, not appear – on his gangplank he was to pay them no attention, but sail with the next tide.

"But, Mysir," Corius burst out, "though I agree with you that he is an honest man enough, will he risk the damage to his trade? And how shall he be paid? Merchant captains do not often act from charity, and it is the nature of being a Personalist in this city that one will be impoverished, for we are barred from advancement in most professions if our sympathies are known."

I muttered a reply regarding certain resources I possessed in Calaria.

Corius began to protest again, for he knew my situation, but his father hushed him. "Mysir Bass has done well to arrange this, and I only hope that we do not need it. Bear in mind, though, Mysir, that the costume of the Uncast does not keep one from the sight of the authorities, only from ordinary citizens."

"I had remembered that," I said, "but could think of no better scheme."

"Nor, indeed, can I," he sighed. "Corius, there is a small community of fugitive Personalists in Calaria already, is there not?"

"There is," he said. "I have spoken with them."

"Then at least they will not be without friends to take them in, if it comes to it. If anything would be worse than being an exile it would be being a friendless exile. Though better that than what might happen to them here."

We fell into a disconcerted silence, and Felkior, uncharacteristically, fidgeted with his half-mask, running his long fingers over it and tapping it with his fingernails – a noticeable sound amid the stillness. Corius looked up incuriously at it, then I saw his eyes widen behind his mask, then contract again as he frowned in thought.

"Father," he said, "would your brother listen to a warning from you?"

"We have not spoken in over twenty years."

"I – am not sure that is an answer to my question," Corius said, in his inimitable combining of deference with impudence.

His father stared at him. "It is a theoretical question only, in any case," he replied, "for I could not get within five hundred paces of him."

"Not as yourself, nay," said Corius. "But this is, after all, the City of Masks. He himself spends his life promoting the belief that the mask is the man."

A small, slow smile began upon the lips of Felkior. "Listen to the boy, Tam," he said, and Tamas's head twitched toward his friend and employer suddenly as he heard the contraction of his name.

"You have not called me Tam since our youth," he said.

"Then it is time to revisit our youth," replied Felkior. "Our youth, when we dared any escapade, when no place in the city was too dangerous or too difficult for us to visit."

"Felkior," said Tamas, "we were much younger then. Also, as I recall we visited mostly boudoirs, not the Temple of the Sun."

"We did not visit the Temple of the Sun because nobody would have tried to keep us out of it and there was nothing there we wanted. You were a priest there, after all. Now the situation is reversed; probably if we tried to visit a boudoir nobody would pay any mind, for we would be no threat, but the Temple of the Sun is forbidden ground."

His smile had flowered fully, and he was digging in a drawer, seeking with his fingers for some item. He pulled it out with a cry of triumph, "Ha!", and turned from us for a moment. When he turned back he wore a different mask. It was a black silk half-vizard, with a silken band which had once been deep red but was now faded to a dark pink. It was decorated with broken hearts of gold and rapiers of steel, and more faded ribbons in primary colours were stitched along the bottom of the mask. It covered half his face, and that half of his face was the man who stood before us as he had been decades before, at the age of perhaps nineteen. He had run his hands through his hair, and white though it was and receding from his forehead, it stood out in wild locks around his head and added to the impression of a daring adventurer.

His age-spotted hands held another mask, in all ways similar except that it was full-face, and with his uncanny ability to locate people despite his blindness he tossed it underhand directly at Tamas, who caught it by reflex and stared at it.

"Felkior," he said, "you are insane."

"Put on the mask and tell me that."

"Felkior – "

"Put on the mask."

Slowly, he lifted the mask to his face. Corius looked aside, as one would if a man were changing his trousers, and I hastened to follow his example as I recalled the customs of the city regarding masklessness. When we looked back, a different man sat in the chair, a younger man, more upright and alert.

"Felkior," said Tamas from behind the mask, "how shall we do this? Have you a plan?"

"We will adopt the garb of junior Sunpriests," said Felkior, and his voice was firm and clear. "Juliana can make up the robes, can she not?" he asked Corius, who concurred. "We will enter the Temple, which you know well, and make our way towards your brother's quarters during the time that we know he will be in there preparing."

"Yes," whispered Tamas.

"The robes will be reversible," Felkior went on, warming to his plotting, excitement growing in his voice. "Inside they will be those of more senior priests, such as would have access to the Archpriest. We reverse the robes, intimidate the attendants, and gain entry."

"The attendants will know all the senior priests."

"We can be foreign or something. Details. Do not interrupt. Once inside, we overpower Benor and gag him. You take his robes and mask."

"I?"

"You are the one who looks like him, are you not? Does he not have an acolyte? Can we get Corius in as well?"

Corius looked less than delighted at his sudden inclusion in the plot, and would have protested if he could have found a pause to speak into, but Felkior did not provide one.

"We will work something out about that. He must have a secret passage or a back door to get his mistresses in and out, if we can find that we may not need the senior priest robes except as a diversion. And we gag the real acolyte, too. We will need to take our swords in under our robes, of course. Then you go out to the ceremony, carrying the Sunmask. No, Corius carries the Sunmask, it is heavy – real gold. I wonder if we could steal it afterwards? In any case, once you reach the courtyard you do the first part of the rite, I am sure you remember, and then the sermon. You had better have a sermon prepared. The sermon is important, because that is how you tell the Personalists that it is you in the robes, not Benor."

"How…"

"We can figure something out. No interruptions, I have a flow here. The Personalists abort their plot. We will need to arrange for a distraction at this point, perhaps some fruit-throwing after all. Under cover of the confusion you and your acolyte – Corius – leave the courtyard and re-enter the temple. Once inside and in some convenient space, you change robes and masks. I wonder if we *can* steal the Sunmask? It would be worth a lot, melted down, and we could distribute the gold among the people of the Moon, that would be appropriate after all. I make my escape out the secret passage and rejoin you. And there we are."

We were all a little stunned to hear the elderly Keeper transformed into the wild youth he had been so many years before. I was the first to speak.

"And do I have a role in your plot, Felkior?"

"Ah, Bass. Yes, an important one. You must stand in the crowd and spread the idea that the man in the Archpriest's robes is not the Archpriest. In particular, you must spread it to Bardo and his men."

We all looked dubiously at Felkior, unsure of our ability to bring off such a plot, despite his air of complete confidence. Frankly, the plan sounded insanely risky, just the kind of foolishness that a nineteen-year-old blade would invent. But when we thought of the alternatives it was something that we had to try, and I said this last aloud.

"Indeed," said Corius. "Indeed. Better a plan like this than no plan at all. But if you will forgive me, it needs considerable work as regards the details."

"Oh, yes, I know," said Felkior airily. "One moment." He turned aside and switched masks again. "Now let us sit down and work out a better plan, one that might succeed," he said, and his voice was deeper and slower, his entire mien altered, as if four or five decades had descended upon him inside a second.

Secret passages, in the end, were indeed the key. There were at least three that Tamas (now also back in his Secretary mask) knew of from the days when he had continually broken curfew from the Temple to roister and run foolish risks with young Felkior. He also, to my surprise, knew several courtesans — to my surprise until he explained that they were among the groups most often given to the Moon faith. "Tomorrow is the full moon," he said, "and I will see them; I can ask them for details of the entrances to the Archpriest's chambers, for if they have not been there themselves then earlier generations certainly have. I think my brother's tastes are catered for among the personnel of the Temple itself, but I know his predecessor was a whoremonger of considerable appetite, and such useful knowledge will have been preserved. All the better, indeed, that the passage not have been used lately, for it will not be borne in mind by any one, and we may the more easily make use of it without detection."

"You go to a service in honour of the Moon tomorrow?" I asked. "Would it be permissible for me to come?"

"Certainly, Bass," he said, "but why?"

"My late mother, and my younger sister, with whom I am close, are – or were, in my mother's case – Moon devotees, for in my country most women follow that faith, and it is not forbidden them," I said. "I have on occasion attended services with them and gained some peace of mind thereby, and peace of mind is somewhat of which I find myself sorely in need. Also, though I am not a man who practices much religion, before such an undertaking I wish to pray; and to do so in the Temple of the Sun would seem inappropriate in the circumstances."

"Indeed," Tamas replied with a smile. "Well, come here as usual tomorrow for your sword lesson, and afterwards we shall to the celebration of the Moon's fullness."

"You may see my sister there," put in Corius. "She goes sometimes."

His words gladdened me, for I had wished to see Juliana again.

I go now to my sword lesson, and will update tonight's events tomorrow.

The twenty-second of the second month

Last night, when the fencing was at an end and our attire changed to that of the Uncast, Tamas took from a concealed cupboard a small case of pale wood with brass corners and a lock, and secreted it under his robes.

"What is that?" I asked. "Or may I not know?"

"You may know, Bass, though I would tell few. Have you wondered, perhaps, how we manage the rites of the Moon in secret, when the time and place of rising is a significant part of the liturgy?"

"I had not wondered it, but now I do."

"This box contains the answer. Clockwork of cunning make, and a compass to align it, and it will tell us precisely of the rising. To possess such a thing is evidence of subversion and heresy."

We descended the stairs and exited the door, and must perforce cease our discussion lest we be overheard; yet I wondered at the sanity of a place in which a device to tell of the movements of the moon, that one might worship, was evidence that one was an enemy of good order and deserved to die.

We went by the low ways, for the Moon people meet in a cellar. I thought for a minute we were going to be robbed on the way, for a footpad stepped from a dark alley and began to draw a knife, but Tamas flashed him some finger-sign and he stepped back and vanished. "The Moon has her dark side," was all his comment.

One or two of the Moon devotees are, by their dress, great ladies (even cloaked anonymously, the cloth is good), but they descend to the dark cellar with the rest when they worship, for the poor cannot rise to the High Paths. Though they must be the financial support of the small community, they are not seated prominently or in any other way distinguished. At the door, each person takes a Moon medallion (a full moon for last night's celebration), for it is too risky to carry them upon their persons – and the ladies take the same pewter disks as the rest.

The walls of the cellar were damp, and for this reason, as well as for their safety, the congregation was closely cloaked. When they entered, they were mainly masked as the Uncast, but that they might participate in the service they assumed the ritual masks of worshippers of the Moon. I myself wore the mask of the Innocent Man, lest I offend some custom inadvertently.

Tamas must set up the clockwork device beneath the silvered disk and lamp that was the Moon's image, upon a small, battered table into which it fitted, and check the alignment by the compass. He handed me off, therefore, to Juliana, who was another of the early arrivals. She was dark-cloaked like the rest, but under her cloak wore her characteristic pale green with a touch of lace.

We greeted each other and inquired as to one another's health. She looked, and said that she was, somewhat better than when last I had seen her, having colour to her cheeks which was pleasant to see. I inquired as to whether Corius had visited her this afternoon (it being his half-day), and she said he had, and had told her that I would be attending the Moon-temple, and therefore she had made sure to be here, "for I did enjoy our talk – if so I can call it, for Sallia did almost all the talking."

I smiled, and enquired after her foster-sister. Was she well? Would she attend the Temple?

"She is well – Bardo is good for her, for all his concentration on his plots he still finds time for her, and I think his affection genuine; and this has helped her to overcome her grief. She lived with Mende, you know, and saw her daily, so it was the greater shock to lose her. But nay, she will not be here. She is very conventional and would not attend a Moon-temple. Besides, would you confide a secret location to Sallia?" This was said with a smile of affection; Juliana, I think, cares deeply for her foolish friend, no less because of her chatter.

"I would not – though many, you know, think me no less a fool than Sallia, and Tamas has done me the honour to trust me with the secret."

"Oh, it is not that she is a fool, just that she cannot but speak of whatever crosses her mind. I wonder sometimes that Bardo dares be with her, but he tells her nothing of his plots and never makes arrangements to meet her; she only knows in a vague way that he is involved in the underground, and never thinks about that, for it is unconventional. But Mysir, you do yourself an injustice in comparing yourself to her; you are, I am sure, as discreet and intelligent a man as befits an envoy, and Tamas is quite right to trust you."

"Alas, though I am a man of honour and would not betray a confidence, still I am of no great intellect. Your brother has tutored me patiently in the Book of Masks, yet I had to ask him what yours signified, for I could not make it out unaided."

"And he told you, of course, that this is the mask of a Courtesan," she said – then gave a small, mischievous, but not unkind laugh at my shock. "I am teasing, Mysir. I am as he told you, an honest if somewhat underemployed Costumier, and as virtuous as one can be and still break the law by attending an illegal temple. Indeed, moreso than my conventional foster-sister, who has a lover – though I must confess that that it is not only through virtue that I lack one."

"Why, Mistress Juliana, what is it you mean? Are you a vowed innocent of the Moon, perhaps?"

She laughed. "Hardly. Nay, Mysir, it is my misfortune to be plain."

"I hardly think so," said I, but at this moment a soft bell was rung repeatedly to signify the commencement of the service, and I had no opportunity to expand upon my remark.

We shared a liturgy book between us, there being few copies. The liturgy of the Moon in Bonvidaeo differs at a number of minor points from that which I had sometimes attended in Calaria, and the print in the liturgy book being something small and in an old-fashioned character, I had to lean close to her to read it. She has a pleasant, cleanly scent, as one who washes regularly, and with herbs.

It being full moon, the liturgy began with the Lady Rising Bright, just as at New Moon it ends with her Rising Dark. It is a kindly service, my favourite of the Moon liturgies, and I found myself much comforted thereby.

"Mistress of the Rising Tide,

Draw up in us the ocean of our tears for those who mourn, especially Tamas and Juliana," said the priestess at one point, and indeed I found my eyes moist for them and for their loss. We shared a glance, Juliana and I, and a tear for her mother slipped from beneath her mask.

"Borrower of the Light,

Lend to us the light of faith,

That dimly we may see our way ahead.

Treader of the Bright Path,

Lead us upon the way,

That as you are renewed, we may be renewed."

"Be it so," we responded.

After the closing blessing, and the ringing of the bell three times, several women of the congregation came to where we were to embrace and sympathise with Juliana, and I began to move aside. She caught my hand, however, and said, "Mysir, do not go. Caria, this is Mysir Bass, my brother's master, who has been most kind to us."

They greeted me, but their concern was with Juliana, and I stood by feeling foolish and out of place as they fussed around her. At length Tamas joined me, having packed up his box and conferred with several women, and we spoke briefly; then Juliana tore herself from the arms of the women and embraced the old man, calling him "Father". The women dispersed, seeing that she was paying all her attention now to Tamas, and she called quick thanks after them and turned to me, her arm still around her father.

"I thank you, Mysir Bass, for bearing me company during the service; it was a pleasure. Perhaps I shall see you again soon, for

I believe my father and Felkior require my services in their mad scheme."

"Do you think it mad?" I asked.

"I think everything that happens in this city mad. I have not seen a sane man or woman, save yourself, in longer than I can say," she said with some bitterness. "And even you, Mysir, participate in the madness of my brother, my father and the good Keeper, though I daresay it is only out of friendship."

I hardly knew what to say to this, and sensing my discomfort, Tamas laughed, embraced his daughter and kissed her cheek, and said to her, "Now, Juliana, if you speak such cynicism we will start calling you Corius next. Say goodnight now to Mysir Bass, for I must take him to his home, where doubtless your brother awaits his safe arrival."

"Good night, Mysir," she said, "travel safely beneath the moon, and greet Corius for me."

"Juliana," I said and bowed, "a good night and safe travel to you also."

"Mysir, you will turn my head with your bowing," she said; "you will be kissing my hand next, if I encourage you."

"Cease your flirting, child," said her father with mock sternness, "and let us go, for there are patrols in the Cloth Way and I wish to avoid them."

"I must go also," said she. "Good night, Father, be well," and with a swift kiss upon his seamed cheek she darted for one of the several exits from the cellar. We took a different exit which led to another street, and – pausing on the way to let a patrol pass – we returned to my home, where Corius was indeed awaiting me with a warm drink to chase the chill of the night. I conveyed to him greetings from his sister and said she had looked well, for which he thanked me.

And so bed, but I did not sleep well, for I do not on bright moonlit nights, and I turned the evening's words over in my mind until at last I fell to sleep and into confused and restless dreams which I now do not remember.

Tonight to the old men as usual for swordplay; I begin to learn some footwork now, but it is slow. Corius departed about an errand, concerning which he was mysterious, and not long afterwards Juliana arrived with her costumier's bag to measure and fit the requisite robes for the imposture at the temple. For lack of a superior plan we are to proceed, and I feel, I confess, a quiver in my digestion at the prospect. So much can go wrong; so easily could it become a bloodbath. I face the prospect of using my sword in earnest, though it be only in self-defence.

Corius has said he will recruit some youths to cause a distraction at his signal. He has discovered somewhat which is better than fruit: a number of wasps' nests, which he will secure in bags and which his youths will hurl broadcast at a critical juncture. His hope is that the broil of the wasps, rudely awakened from their winter sleep, will distract nearby persons sufficiently to prevent them from fighting. Having once stumbled upon a wasps' nest I must concur with his assessment. They will also prevent the youths from being seized upon, likewise a crucial aspect of his plan.

Tamas spoke to one of the older courtesans last night, while I was engaged with Juliana, who had been familiar with the previous Archpriest and knew the secret way into his quarters. It departs, in fact, from the back of a house which has been a famous disreputable house for many years, and which has, as all such houses, discreet entrances from minor streets. "Send your young man to us," he reported her as saying, "and we will put him on the right way and show him the secret passage – and the one to the Temple as well."

I will confess I do not understand the distinction she was making, but Juliana laughed. "And will you send Corius, then, when he returns?"

"Not tonight, I think," said her father, "for this is the house's busy time. During the day would be far better; in the morning, best of all. We do not wish him to encounter a member of the conspiracy, for example."

"Nor one of the priests," put in Felkior. I was somewhat shocked at their assumption that the vows of the Sunpriests meant nothing to them; it is not so in our land, I am sure.

"Well, it will be a new experience for Corius," said his sister, "or so I hope, at least. I cannot stay to greet him, which I regret, for I would like to see his face when you tell him of his mission. That is all the measurements, I think; I will have the robes for you tomorrow. Nay, I do not need measurements for Corius, for I have made his clothes for years and know them exactly. Fare you well, Father, Felkior – Mysir Bass," and she bobbed me a low curtsey and smiled at me, then trotted down the stairs.

Shortly afterwards her brother returned. "Corius," I said, "you have missed your sister, though not by a great deal."

"Nay, Mysir, I have not," he said; "I have just encountered her and she has given me her news. She took delight in acquainting me with my destination tomorrow morning, the mischief. She is in want of steadying."

"While you, of course, are cautious and never do anything headstrong or ill-considered," remarked his father with a laugh, to which Corius returned a smile. It was gratifying to me to see the affection that had always been between these two become more open, now that their relationship was acknowledged; likewise the affection he had given and received with Juliana the previous night, for it is my belief that he may have led a life in which simple human affection has played too small a part. "But it is true," he said, "that she is in want of steadying; she was flirting most shamefully last night and I had to rebuke her for it."

"With whom?" said Corius. "Ought I to warn him off?"

"I do not think you ought," said Tamas; "it was with your master."

"Mysir Bass! I do apologise on my sister's behalf," said Corius, "she ought not to do so."

"Indeed," said I, "there is nothing to forgive, for I detected nothing improper in her conduct," though as I said it I felt that this was not, perhaps, in all ways true.

"You are too polite, Mysir," said my servant. "She ought to remember your relative social positions, and conduct herself with more discretion."

"Well, as to our relative positions," I said, "let us see. My father was a wealthy landowner, but untitled; I am the second son, and possess but a life interest in a farm, the income from which, in the days when I worked in the capital of Calaria, did little more than cover the rent on my town dwelling. I have my income as an Envoy, which for a post such as Bonvidaeo is not generous; I am an honest man, and the various supplements which others make to their stipends I feel compelled to decline. My father in his second marriage wed a granddaughter of nobility – whose father was a younger son. Their daughter, my half-sister, also is married to a younger son of a noble house, who by an unexpected chance arising through a scandal in government, combined with family connections on his distaff side, found himself advanced to be Undersecretary to the new Foreign Minister. By his influence, or her influence with him, I was able to enter the government service. I had wished to serve my country, and my eyesight being poor I was unable to enter the Army or Navy, as is usually the lot of younger sons who lack the intelligence needed in the law or the Temple. Unable to bring myself to participate in the vulgar brawl for advancement which is the true condition of the so-called public service, I did not rise. At length I was given Bonvidaeo, which was praised to me as an important post, yet though I am a fool and short-sighted, I am neither imbecilic nor entirely blind. Your pardon, Master Keeper."

"No offence taken," replied the good old man.

"On the other side, we have the acknowledged daughter of a good man of noble blood, attainted by the state for what I must confess I cannot bring myself to see as a crime – that of possessing his own conscience. Certainly she was born outside wed-lock, and to a woman of the servant classes, but history is replete with persons whose parents, for many reasons, did not wed and who nonetheless are honoured for their accomplishments. She is intelligent, well-educated, discreet and, I think, courageous; good-humoured and of a pleasant appearance. If she wishes – which I do not, by the way, believe – to – " I struggled for a way of conveying my meaning.

"Flirt?" suggested Corius.

"Pay attention to?" – his father.

"Love?" – Felkior, and we all turned to look at him. Then:

"If she considers me in such a way," I concluded at last, "I am hardly in a position to object on the grounds of her ancestry, or on any other grounds."

"Are you saying you – like my sister?" said Corius after a silence. There was a note of challenge in his voice.

"I have the greatest respect, liking and fondness for your sis-ter, on our short acquaintance," I replied with dignity, "and wish that acquaintance to deepen. But I have no dishonourable inten-tions towards her, if such is your concern."

"Mysir," he said, "that would always be my last concern, with you."

This unanticipated tribute silenced me, and after an awkward moment Felkior turned the discussion to what was a more pressing matter, that of our plans for the Solstice service, now only a day and a half distant.

We talked late and it is later now, and tomorrow is another day of planning – for the day of preparation for the Solstice is a holiday in the City, and our office is closed. So I will cease now and go to sleep as best I may.

The twenty-third of the second month

Corius went off this morning to scout the secret passage; afterwards, he said, he would contact his young helpers and show them the wasps' nests, so we should not expect him back before the early afternoon. Late in the morning Juliana came; she had not the robes with her, for they were not yet finished (they were in the hands of seamstresses she had reason to trust, from the Moon Temple), but she came, she said, to see us all before we should face the dangers of the morrow.

"The day after Solstice is a holiday also," she said; "if we are all still living and hale, let us agree to meet then and spend it together, drinking mulled wine perhaps before this fire, and speaking of only pleasant matters." Her eyes were on me as she said this.

"Nothing would give me more pleasure," I replied, with entire honesty.

"I look forward to it, Mysir Bass," she said, and I replied, "It would please me, Juliana, if you could call me Gregorius sometimes."

"Gregorius," she said, and smiled. "The name suits you. Thank you, I will do so."

She had to go, to check upon the seamstresses, ere Corius returned. He reported the passage very dusty, but intact and easily traversable. There was a spyhole at the end whence one could observe the Archpriest's quarters; he described the room minutely, and it accorded with Tamas's memories except in minor details such as might have been changed since he saw it last, so we knew we had the correct location. He had carefully opened the door at the end to ensure that this could be done easily, "and it was as well, for the hinges were very stiff. I returned for oil, and they now move much more smoothly – also silently, which is much to our purpose." Nobody was there, preparations for the service being in train throughout the day, and the Archpriest being required elsewhere.

The boys had greeted the prank of the wasps with much enthusiasm, and volunteered the location of still more nests, so that most of them would have two nests each to hurl; the confusion would be most satisfactory. The wasps being dormant at this time of year, the nests could easily be captured in the calico sacks which Corius supplied, and the boys themselves had proposed carrying a brazier to the rooftop whence they planned to launch their assault, to warm them so that the insects were the more mobile upon their sudden release out of the sacks.

"It is well," said Felkior. "Now, Corius, you must listen to the sermon we have written for your father. What is the signal you have agreed with the boys?"

"I shall drop the Sunmask," he replied.

"Excellent," he said, "and most appropriate. We shall plan at what point to do so when you have listened to the sermon. It would be well, perhaps, if Tamas were to cuff you as you attempt to pick up the mask, to pursue you, then, within the temple ahead of the crowd fleeing the wasps, and then for you to dart together into the lesser oratory's small alms-office and turn your robes."

Corius agreed to this, and listened attentively and with appreciation to the sermon. We had abandoned, by now, the ploy of attempting to convey to the listening Personalists that Tamas was not in fact the Archpriest, as too difficult to achieve while not arousing the suspicions of the Temple functionaries who would surround him. "Besides," Corius had argued, "it will not matter to Bardo who is in the mask. Personalist or not, he will want to assassinate whoever puts on the mask, and if you walked up to him and told him to his face who you were, it would not stop him." So our plan hinged upon putting a stop to the proceedings before the "Archpriest" should assume the mask at all, and so foiling Bardo's intent by giving him no opportunity – while preserving the appearance that it was the Archpriest who had appeared.

This did not prevent the creation of a sermon with a degree of irony, however, and such was the speech which the old men together had produced. I asked them for a copy to include in my journal, and shall do so in its proper place in the entry for tomorrow. (I reassured them that my journal is written in a cipher, for they were somewhat perturbed that I was keeping one.)

I pray that I be spared to make tomorrow's journal entry. For although I no longer have the task – as Corius contended, impossible – of convincing the assassins not to strike, still our plan places me in the crowd, to give warning if I see a crossbow raised. I am to sit upon a stepladder (the better to see – not the ceremony, as I would pretend, but the crowd), and feign to drink wine and be a merry plump fool, for I will be masked on this occasion as the Innocent Man.

"Remember, though," said Tamas with great emphasis, "to carry the Gentle Knight's mask, and to pull it on over the lamb-swool if so be you need to take action, for the Innocent Man with a sword will be arrested forthwith, regardless of circumstances."

I promised that I would remember.

One of the seamstresses came as we ate our belated evening meal, bearing the robes, good wishes from Juliana, and, for me, a token.

"Mistress Juliana said, would you wear this for her on the morrow," said the tiny seamstress, who put me in mind in every way of a small brown bird – her bright eye, her swift movements, and her constantly bobbing head, crowned with brown hair just the colour of her dress. I thanked her, and pinned it within my coat – a small weaving of such ribbons as are used upon the borders of masks. I did not inquire from my companions as to its exact significance, and they did not volunteer remarks or indeed appear to take any notice in particular.

Tonight we contrived to go to bed early, and if we dared, both Corius and I would have taken of his sleeping draught, but that we must wake well before dawn. For dawn farther south comes sooner, even at this midwintertide, than in my home, where but three hours of daylight before and after noon can be expected at this time of year.

The twenty-eighth of the second month

I have not been able to update this journal since the astonishing events of Solstice, but now I must begin to set them down in good order, though I do not think that I will finish today. Juliana does not permit me to tire myself and she will come and take the pen from me if she thinks I write too long.

We rose several hours before dawn and met the old men at their house, where we went over the plan for the final time, checking each aspect from lists which Tamas the secretary had prepared. There was another gift from Juliana for each of us: a kind of very light armour in the form of a tabard. It consisted of several layers of thickly braided, stiff canvas backed with leather, and would protect us from collarbone to thigh beneath our robes or, in my case, beneath my heavy cloak. It was in part, her note said, from our friends the mercers, who had made it to her measure and design when she had hinted that we were at risk of attack from the Butcher. I was at first annoyed by what I saw as her deception, until Corius reminded me of his prediction that the Butcher would attack a priest that very night, when three of us would be going robed as priests. It was warm, also, which did not go amiss, for the night was as cold and damp – and dark – as one would anticipate of midwinter.

The moon had set, and we carried a tin lantern with a door which we could close if we looked like encountering the Watch. (In Bonvidaeo, anyone wandering the night who is caught up by the Watch will be released if he can satisfy them that his Character permits or requires such nocturnal adventures – at least, such is the theory. In practice one must also pay a bribe, and it may be a somewhat drawn-out and argumentative process. It is preferable, therefore, to avoid the Watch in the first instance. Fortunately they were travelling in still larger and noisier groups than usual, with an abundance of light, ever since their comrade had met his death at the hands of the Butcher, so avoiding them was even less difficult than was normally the case.)

Corius, Tamas and Felkior wore dark cloaks over their priests' robes, which they would remove at the entrance to the tunnel and retrieve at their leisure. I parted from them at one of the side entrances to the house; we skulked in a nearby alley while a slender young courtesan, consulting a slip of paper in her hand, exited from the door and made her way up a set of stairs to the main street level. She passed close to us, carrying a light, and when she had gone Corius whispered to us, "Late callout. She had a map with a red line." Apparently this is the manner of making discreet assignations outside the houses, to send in a hired messenger with a sketch map without words upon it (that one's writing may not be recognized – and besides, most of the girls cannot read), the point of departure and the route marked in red. One then intercepts the young woman somewhere along the route and she accompanies one to one's chosen spot, hooded and blindfolded for the last part of the journey. She therefore knows neither one's name, one's address nor, naturally, one's face. So Felkior told me in whispers, somewhat in the manner of a man who reminisced of his youth, I felt. Then he clasped my hand and wished me well, and they knocked a prearranged signal upon the portal and vanished inside.

I felt my aloneness keenly as I hastened to the place where we had agreed with the youths that they would assemble. Some were late, and I spoke sharply to them in my nervousness; I gained the impression that they generally did not rise so early, though they might seek their beds at such a time. I distributed the part-payment we had agreed upon (Corius had given them somewhat when they were recruited, I gave them a second fee upon their assembly and a third was owed them upon successful completion of their mission of distraction). They were burdened with their sacks of wasps and with two portable braziers and some charcoal to warm the insects from their dormant state. I had some string bags of chestnuts also, a last-minute addition of Corius's to give a colour of legitimacy and innocence to their braziers should they be observed, and these were greeted cheerfully as I distributed them. "Remember," I cautioned them, "when the Sunmask is dropped, throw the wasps as far and as hard as you are able, into the square in the direction of the priests on the steps."

They assured me, with some impertinence, that they would remember. Then they, too, left me. They would ascend to the roofs and make their way cautiously to a house among those lining the avenues which surround the temple – for it is similarly situated to the palace, surrounded with open ground, though not so wide – there to set up where the slope of the roof would hide their preparations from those below.

Alone once more and very conscious of it, I collected my stepladder from where Corius had previously secreted it upon the roof of somebody's woodshed ("He will see the chalk mark on it and know not to move it – mind you brush the chalk off, some of the Guard may know the sign"). My bottle was in a canvas bag over my shoulder, which I had also used to carry the chestnuts. As I emerged into the torchlit space, I took care to weave a little, and struggle with the stepladder, which I spoke to sharply as I set it up.

"Stupid – *ladder*. What ill spirit got into you? Hey? Spirit got into someone, anyway!" I said, and laughed raucously at my own humour. "Stay – open, condemn you! Stupid thing," and so forth, as I wrestled with the ladder, dropped it, tripped over it, kicked it, attempted to lean it without opening it properly and had it slip down the wall, opened it upside down and made much owlish difficulty of rotating it, knocked it down again – I had attracted a crowd of onlookers by this time, who were contributing their own commentary and suggestions and gaining great amusement from my struggles. At length I had the ladder the correct way up, open, and stable enough that I might sit upon it without falling off (which I had taken care to do once – I did not repeat it, however, for I landed on my swordhilt and felt it give me a bruise in the ribs even through Juliana's padded coat).

I unshipped my canvas bag with the bottle and, keeping the canvas wrapped around it, took what I feigned to be a hearty pull. "Don't like to see the level dropping," I confided at some volume to a randomly selected member of the observers' circle, pointing at the swathed container. "Clever, eh?" – and I belched pungently into his face. He drew back suddenly, and, once they concluded that the most entertaining part was over, he and his companions dispersed, heading for the good positions they had no doubt risen early to obtain.

The crowd had started to filter into the square, and I noted an unusual preponderance of fit-looking youths who did not give the impression that they normally rose before dawn to attend Temple. All of them wore heavy cloaks, which given the weather was understandable, but I saw some angular devices hidden under those cloaks as the wind blew them close to their bodies. The Guard did not appear to have been alerted; their numbers were no more than one would usually expect and they seemed sleepy and ill-disciplined. They were stationed at the foot of the temple steps, on which the senior priests would assemble to lead the crowd in the responses, and atop which, under the portico and before the main doors, Tamas would enact the role of his brother the Archpriest and officiate over the ceremony.

All going well.

In the interests of narrative I am now going to leave myself in the Square, sipping at my bottle (which was wrapped to conceal the fact that the level was *not* dropping) and scratching or belching at intervals, and report the experience of Corius, Tamas and Felkior after they left me in the low street and entered the house of ill repute. This is their account of what occurred.

They were welcomed by Tamas's coreligionist of the Moon and taken to the back of the house, where the tunnel to the Temple was concealed behind a movable robe-closet in a room itself concealed behind a hanging. The door had a trick lock and no obvious handle – secrecy had clearly been of the essence for the builders of this particular way, but secrets which living people know are not secrets, as they say.

Their black outdoor robes went into the closet, and they entered the tunnel covered in lighter robes to prevent their golden-yellow priests' disguises gathering the dust and cobwebs which infested it. The path was plain to their lantern, for Corius had had the guidance of the middle-aged courtesan who was now in charge of the house, but who in her younger days had frequently been called along the passage, and his earlier footmarks and hers were clear in the dust of the two decades since that time. There were side passages and turnings, the whole forming something of a maze, apparently as a further security measure, since there appeared, the courtesan had informed Corius, to be no other entrances or exits. The passage had been made long before her time, and the first she knew of it was when a map arrived showing the path through the maze in red, and an older courtesan who had served a previous incumbent had shown her the entrance. In the midst of the maze, Tamas told me, was rather a fine erotic sculpture dating from before the suppression of the Moon cult, and depicting the mythic figures of the Sun and Moon.

They had no time to admire this artwork, however, and they hurried forward to the end of the labyrinth, slowing their footsteps only when they reached a scarf which Corius had placed in order to indicate that they were approaching the egress.

They stopped their lantern down to a slit and crept to the door, where Corius checked the peephole, then gestured them further back along the corridor and whispered to them breathily.

"The Archpriest is there but his acolyte is absent. We may have to wait."

They nodded and crept back, Corius and Tamas leading blind Felkior, all of them in the Young Felkior mask. Tamas and Corius took turns of a few minutes each, watching through the hole; it was a single hole and one had to close one eye and press the other against the chill stone, a process made more difficult by their masks. At length the acolyte returned, bearing warm water wherewith to wash his principal's feet.

As he was engaged in this task, father and son slipped silently through the carefully oiled door concealed behind the arras which lined the palatial chamber. Tamas, having squeezed Felkior's arm to signal "stay here," indicated by inclining his head that he would move left and Corius right. This was the most risky part of the whole venture, for if someone else opened the door at the critical moment, or either party cried out loudly, they would be discovered and would be fortunate to escape with their lives, let alone put their plan into effect. The stone walls blocked most sound, but a loud enough cry might escape.

By the creaking of the chair and the splashing of the water, they could tell that their targets had not changed position. The boy was kneeling on their right, Corius's side, with his left hand towards them, and Benor the Archpriest sat facing him. The two attackers would each be coming at their targets from one side and slightly behind.

When they reached the ends of the arras, by prearrangement they looked back, and Corius, whose left hand was innermost, gave the count of three on his fingers, then they plunged together at the startled Temple denizens. Corius, leaving his sword sheathed, tackled the youth and knocked him from his knees, wrapping his right hand equipped with a rag around the acolyte's mouth and shoving the gag home when he opened his mouth to yell or bite. The acolyte choked, and Corius pulled his unresisting hands up behind him and planted a knee in the small of his back.

Meanwhile, Tamas had stepped out, levelling his sword, and said in a low voice, "Don't move or call out, Benor."

The startled Archpriest drew in a breath, thought better of crying out, and let it out again. "Tamas," he said quietly. "It has been a long time."

Felkior stepped out from behind the arras at this juncture, and the Archpriest's eyes widened. "And your friend," he said. "Revisiting your youth?"

"You could say that," said Felkior.

"Do you intend to kill me?" asked Benor, eyeing Corius's efficient trussing up of his acolyte.

"You ought to know me better than that," said Tamas.

"I probably ought, although given that the last time we spoke was almost twenty years ago, you will forgive me for being unaware of your current philosophical position as regards the killing of brothers."

"Come over here and bind and gag him too," said Tamas, addressing Corius, who had secured the sobbing acolyte adequately for the moment. They had agreed that Corius's name was not to be used in Benor's hearing.

"Anything for the last word, eh, brother?"

Tamas regarded him with distaste while Corius did a much more thorough job of binding and gagging than he had with the acolyte, then returned to that youth and completed his work.

"Now," said Tamas, "we are going to slide you under the bed where you will be out of the way, and leave Felkior to look after you while we take care of some business for which your presence is unrequired. Where is – ah."

Juliana's seamstresses had made only the robes of an acolyte and the underrobes of the Archpriest, for the full Winter Solstice robes of the Archpriest were elaborate in the extreme, a rich crimson decorated with yards of gold braid and intricate symbolic embroidery, and they would, of course, be in the Archpriest's chambers, ready for him to assume. This, with Corius's assistance, he now did. His brother had gained more weight than he in recent years, but Juliana had provided padding accordingly, and once he had assumed the equally elaborate mask of the Archpriest his resemblance to Benor was exact. While Corius was distinguishable from Benor's acolyte on close examination, they were sufficiently confident that nobody would look closely at an acolyte and that he would pass in the dim lighting of Solstice morning.

The mask of the Archpriest is distinct from the Sunmask, which precious object was kept in the Temple treasury and handed over to the Archpriest's acolyte in the Archpriest's presence immediately prior to the ceremony. Accordingly, at the appropriate stroke of the bell, they left Felkior guarding the bound, gagged and blindfolded prisoners whom they had shoved beneath the Archpriest's enormous bed and made their way forward from the living quarters to the front of the temple, proceeding at a stately pace to collect this ultimate symbol of the god.

Meanwhile, back in the avenue fronting the Temple, the crowd was thickening and I was glad of my stepladder, which enabled me to see what was going on. A guardsman had wandered over to inspect me briefly, but when he saw my mask and heard my cheerfully fuddled greeting he lost interest and sheered off.

The most minor of the priests who would be taking part in the ceremony were now spilling out of the Temple, to take their places on the lowest steps. This included the boys and men of the choir, who began warming up their voices – no easy task in such weather and at such an hour, especially since their robes are of a relatively thin white stuff which leaves them shivering. The Guard had to discourage certain festive citizens who had their own versions of the hymns from singing them in competition, and I saw several drunks, not protected by the mask of the Innocent Man, hauled off and ejected from the area. I reduced my monologue to mumbling as a precaution.

The quantity of large young men was really very marked by now, and I marveled at the stupidity of the Guard. No doubt if our plan failed, they would pay for their lack of alertness with their lives, for I saw some of the probable assassins tracking their movements; it seemed likely that they had been assigned to dispatch them when the shooting started, to prevent their belated interference. Above me, too, in the balconies which were rented on these occasions to people who wanted a good view of the proceedings, youth and masculinity was much in evidence. Appropriate enough for a celebration of the Sun in one way, but I did not think that this was the reason for their presence. The boys had been instructed to drop wasps' nests into the balconies also, but whether they would remember in the excitement of the moment, or be able to target them accurately, very much remained to be seen and we were not relying upon it.

With a shock, I recognized Bardo himself in the crowd, standing not far ahead of me. He was dangling a sailor's signaling pipe from a cord in his left hand, and I began to wonder whether it would bring about triumph or disaster to slip up behind him and wrench it from his grasp. I eventually concluded that it would bring disaster, since he doubtless had voice commands prepared also.

The choir began another hymn – the haunting *Our Lord is Now in Darkness* – and the crowd quieted as the senior priests filed out and occupied the upper steps. Exactly at the end of the hymn, a final figure in the robes of the Archpriest, attended by an acolyte who carried the Mask of the Sun, emerged and took up his post in the portico, between the altar of flame on his right and the perch of the sacred eagle on his left. I strained my inadequate eyes, but could not determine if the acolyte was Corius.

There was a general shifting in the crowd in the silence after the hymn, and I noticed a number of the large young men checking beneath their coats. I could only hope that, firstly, Corius's information was correct and they would wait until the Sunmask was on the Archpriest before launching their assassination attempt, and secondly, that these were in fact Corius and Tamas, who would not put it on.

The responses began, led by the Archpriest in a clear voice which certainly sounded like that of Tamas, but I assumed that I would not be able to tell his brother's voice from his. I had to wait in suspense until the commencement of the sermon before I could be sure. I noted a few differences from our northern practice, notably that at key points a secondary priest would cast small quantities of powder into the altar flame and cause it to flare up brightly and emit vivid sparks.

For the sermon, a small portable lectern was brought and placed before the Archpriest to rest his notes upon. I hoped for a moment that it might be substantial enough to protect him, but the wood looked thin and I suspected that a crossbow bolt would hardly be slowed by it. He began to speak, and at the end of the first sentence I relaxed somewhat, for the words were those I had heard in Felkior's house, at a time which now seemed much longer ago than the previous day.

"My brothers and sisters beneath the Sun," he began, "this is the day on which begins our Lord's resurgence, after long retreat before the dark. Each year, we have this opportunity, this reminder, that we too can overcome the darkness within ourselves and outside ourselves, though we may have long retreated before it. Indeed, we have the reminder daily that we can rise, that we can shine out, that we can banish before us the darkness; that we also, heroes of the Sun, can be conquerors.

"It is in opposing evil, my brothers and my sisters, it is in opposing evil, it is in opposing ignorance, it is in opposing what is hidden and bringing it out into the light, that we portray the Lord Sun. At the conclusion of my address I will be taking up the Sunmask, and when I assume it you will say, the Archpriest is portraying the Lord Sun; the Lord Sun is among us. But each one of us can portray the Lord Sun, whatever mask it is that we are wearing, for we put on his mask when we act heroically, when we act in the Light, when we oppose evil and ignorance and what is hidden and false. A mask, say some foreigners and heretics, is a false thing, it is how a person pretends to be what he is not. But a mask can be how a person pretends to be what he is; how he portrays what is in the depths of his heart. And when from the depths of our hearts we act out opposition to evil and ignorance and concealment and subterfuge, then we are wearing the Sunmask, be the mask on our face whatever it may be."

Some of the senior priests were frowning by this time and shifting their feet, uncomfortable with the thrust of the sermon, which was, of course, sophisticated Personalist theology, though they could not be quite sure of it. They had for so long caricatured Personalism that they did not recognise it when they heard it.

"Some might say," said Tamas, sweeping his gaze among the priests, "some might say that what I speak here is heresy, that what a mask portrays is always the reality – but indeed that is what I am saying. For a mask is not merely a construction of wood, paper, silk, metal or whatever materials it is made from. No, a mask is more than that, for how can silk and glue, manipulated by the hands of men, or even beaten gold or indeed any physical substance, be truth itself? A mask is made, not only by the craftsman whose hands have formed its physical being – as parents form our bodies – but by the wearer and by those the wearer encounters – as we, and those we befriend and oppose and learn from, form ourselves as human beings, form our souls.

"The soul is a flame, we are taught, like and yet unlike to this flame which burns beside me; it is a flame which feels, reasons, speaks, forms relationships of love – and also of hatred. And like this flame beside me, it can be seen, and when we make it manifest, we call this a mask. For the mask which hides is not the true mask, it is not the light but the darkness; it is the mask which reveals that is the true mask. This is why, when we honour some man or woman by naming him or her a Character, the mask that is given to him or her is the mask of his or her own face. We are saying: This man has portrayed himself, this woman has portrayed herself. Only his face, or her face, can represent who and what this person is, for he or she has been himself or herself.

"And so I say to you, brothers and sisters, children of the Lord Sun, put on the Sunmask each day in your lives. Take upon yourself the light, not as something merely external to yourself, but as something that rises up from within you, that is the truth of who you are. Each day arise, each year renew yourselves, in the struggle against evil, in the struggle against ignorance, in the struggle to bring truth out where it may be seen. Wear the true mask. Do not have one appearance in your words and another in your actions; be whole. Do not wear the mask of darkness; wear the mask of light. Wear the mask of your own face and let that be the face of the Lord Sun. And if you do so, you too, in your daily lives, in your daily business, in your daily rising and your daily shining, in small ways and in large ways, you will be heroes of the Sun." He paused, and scanned the crowd. The timekeeper signaled to him; they must move on if he was to assume the Sunmask at the moment of sunrise.

"The Light be upon you, children, now and always," he concluded, and the crowd responded (somewhat bemusedly in some cases): "And also upon you."

The choir began another hymn, and again the attendant priest cast a pinch of powder into the flame and brought the rising sparks. The dawn moment was near, and I tensed and adjusted my blade beneath my cloak, holding the winebottle – now out of its bag – loosely in case I had to give the signal we had prearranged. (If I saw a crossbow leveled I was to drop the bottle and smash it as a warning.) But Bardo's discipline over his people held. I saw him fidget with the whistle as the lectern was ceremoniously borne away, as Tamas and Corius moved back slightly in the portico, as Tamas bowed his head and Corius lifted the heavy golden mask and held it until the dawn moment should be signaled by the ringing of a golden bell, as the bellringer poised, his eye upon a timepiece (for the sky was comprehensively overcast). Then Bardo started and the whistle slipped from his fingers and dangled on its cord from his wrist, for Corius dropped the mask with a resounding clang.

He bent to pick it up, and Tamas cuffed him, whereupon he staggered back against the altar of flame. I, forewarned, hid my eyes, but anyone else watching the byplay was momentarily blinded by the flash as he overturned the entire bowl of powder into the flames. Glancing up, I saw everything happening at once: the altarkeeper reeling back; Corius dropping to the marble paving behind the altar and kicking the flashing mask into the middle of the startled priests, who then dived for it and crashed heads; Tamas ducking behind a pillar; a few of the large young men going for their crossbows (I dropped my bottle but its smash went unheard in the confusion); Bardo, wrongfooted, fumbling his whistle to his lips and blowing a signal; and the first volley of canvas sacks from the rooftop, falling to strike the thick crowd and releasing their cargo of enraged wasps.

Within a period of a few seconds, the entire scene was transformed into chaos. Bardo's first signal was evidently "Do not fire, keep your weapons concealed," for those few who had begun to take them out hurriedly concealed them again, with the exception of one not far from me who had taken a direct hit from a wasps' nest and was rushing for one of the archways which gave egress from the plaza. As he passed near me he jostled another cloaked figure – an Uncast – in his haste, and both of them went down, wasps buzzing furiously around them. He dropped his half-drawn crossbow, and the other person also dropped something, a pale object that I could not quite make out – probably a mask, I thought. They scrambled to their feet and fled in different directions, swatting at the wasps and trying to protect their faces.

Nor were they alone, for the second wave of wasps' nests had descended, to the whoops of the boys from above. The Sunpriests' choir had received a sackful in its midst (the boy who threw that bag having achieved a commendable distance, I thought), and their powerful, trained voices were raised in shrieks of pain as they rushed up the steps, shoving their superiors in their haste. The crowd was thinning rapidly as panicked people made for the – fortunately wide and plentiful – exits from the avenue. A few were knocked down and trampled. Few children were present because of the unpleasant weather, of which I was glad; the death of a child is too high a price for anything.

Within what seemed less than a minute, three-quarters of the crowd had vacated the square, and most of those remaining were clustered around Bardo. He had been frantically blowing his whistle to assemble his men, a few more of whom sheepishly returned from the archways and around the corners of the temple as the wasps, made torpid again by the cold and damp, lost their momentum and could be crushed or avoided. The priests had withdrawn into the temple, no doubt in search of their Archpriest, and I could only hope that they did not find him (or anyone impersonating him) for some time.

Various objects were left behind – bags, the occasional piece of clothing – but only one visible crossbow, the one I had seen dropped. I descended from my ladder and hastened over towards it in the hope of concealing this last bit of evidence of the plot, for Bardo's people did not seem to have remarked it. As I approached it, my eye fell upon the mask – for it was a mask – that had been dropped near it by the person the crossbowman had jostled, and my eyes widened until they must have matched those in the sheepskin upon my face.

Felkior had described to all of us the death mask of the Butcher, and the attributes of an ordinary butcher's mask, so that we would recognise the killer if we saw him. The mask before me matched his description exactly, and in an access of emotion I clutched at my face with my hands – and felt the mask of the Innocent Man, the wool rough against my fingers. Pulling out my other mask – for this was the Gentle Knight's moment – I looked around in the direction the jostled person had fled, and saw a cloaked figure climbing an access ladder which led up a wall to the High Paths.

I snatched the fallen crossbow from the ground. The mechanism was still cocked, and three bolts were fastened beneath the stock. I fumbled one out as I hastened towards the fugitive, bellowing over my shoulder, "Bardo! The Butcher!"

I think the fleeing Butcher heard me, for he redoubled his pace. Once I had loaded I fired, for although the range was not good I feared the fugitive would reach the safety of the rooftops. The bolt went high, and the Butcher paused as it smashed above him and to the side, then surged towards the roof again.

I had to stop a moment and use the foot stirrup to re-cock the bow, for I was not quite strong enough to cock it without. Then I hurried towards the ladder, slotting another bolt into place as I made my best pace – not, alas, fast enough to reach the ladder's foot before the fugitive Butcher reached the top. He was outlined briefly against the sky, now beginning to lighten, and I fired again. I could not tell whether the bolt hit or not, as the figure rolled over the roof parapet onto the High Path.

The crossbow would only encumber me in climbing the ladder, so I dropped it and began to haul myself up the firm, well-spaced but somewhat damp wooden rungs, installed at the behest of some noble blade who liked to wander the roofs but required some way to descend into the temple avenue. I am a bulky man, but strong, and I made good time, though I was somewhat winded when I reached the top. Not as winded as I would have been before my lessons with the sword, I thought, and with that unsheathed my blade and hurried in pursuit of the figure I could just see vanishing across a bridge to the next roof. I had seen a sword's shape underneath his cloak as he had been climbing.

Now Juliana says I must stop and continue on the morrow.

The twenty-ninth of the second month

I had not previously walked upon the High Paths, for their use is reserved to the Bonvidaeoan nobility. I was not about to let this custom stop me, however, in pursuit of someone who had murdered five people (if not six, by now, for Corius's theory was that he would kill on the night just gone). Nor did my misliking for heights hinder me. My blood was up, and my sword out, and I would have this Butcher or die in the attempt.

The fleeing figure seemed that of a small man, and I feared at first that I would be outdistanced too quickly and that the fugitive would elude me by his greater agility and rapidity of progress (and a better knowledge of the ways, with which he was evidently familiar). I soon noted, however, some spots of blood upon the Paths, and dared to hope that my second bolt had struck him and might slow his flight. This proved to be the case, for when I reached the edge of the next roof where I had seen him vanish and looked about, he was still visible, and limping noticeably where before he had been whole. This surprised me somewhat, for owing to my eyesight I have never been accurate with a bow (though I remembered my father telling me, "A crossbow is not a gentleman's weapon, for it requires but little skill"). Clearly I had hit him but a glancing blow, however.

The roofing slates of Bonvidaeo are grey – dark grey when they are damp – and the slowly lightening sky was grey also with overcast. Between the two, the black figure fled.

After taking a moment to determine, of the several branches of the Paths, which I needed to follow in order to come up with the Butcher, I pounded forward at my best pace, my footsteps ringing loudly upon the wooden slats with which the Paths are floored. They differ in construction, some well-traveled ways even possessing tiled coverings and handrails, while in other places they are no more than single planks. If one is fortunate, these have slats nailed across them to assist the grip of one's boots, but often enough they are smooth, and treacherous to a hurrying man. The part of the Paths I traversed was medium in this regard, not covered or railed, but several planks in width and, at points where they descended, formed into proper steps. After the rainy night they were damp, and I slipped once and barely prevented myself from a fall off the Paths onto the slope of the roof.

Soon enough in my pursuit, however, the Butcher led me onto narrower and more precipitous ways where my greater speed of movement was nullified by the treacherous footing, and I ceased to gain ground, though I took care (at some risk to myself) not to lose any either. I wished I had contrived somehow to bring the crossbow, for even a shooter such as I could have hit him at such a distance, but I had not, and there was no helping it. I wasted neither time nor breath in crying out for him to halt. It was a pursuit to the finish, and we both knew it.

He, however, was hindered in that he had to keep a watch behind him, while all my focus was before; and, looking back while making his way along a roof-crest, he stumbled on his injured side and fell, barely arresting himself from rolling down the slope of the roof. Rain is less frequent in Bonvidaeo than in Calaria (and snow is unknown), and the slope of the roofs is correspondingly less; still it is enough to cause the heart to thud thinking of sliding down one, and I forbore to put on more speed lest I also should fall. I made the best, however, of my opportunity to close the gap further.

Before long, too, the area of narrow ways ended and he was forced to cross a more popular and hence safer route, where I again gained. I had found a second wind by now, and when we reached a straight stretch four planks in width and in the valley between two roofs, I put on a spurt which carried me almost within reach of him.

Hearing my footfalls pressing him so close, he did not dare look back, but vaulted a rail at the edge of a roof and dropped suddenly to a lower level – hoping, I imagined, that so clumsy a man as I would not dare follow. I heard him cry out as he hit, the injury to his leg no doubt paining him, and this encouraged me to quickly imitate his drop.

For fear, I think, that if I paused I would not have the courage to make the leap, I had not sheathed my sword despite the danger of only having one hand free to catch me if I should slip. I was immediately glad of this decision, for the Butcher had also drawn a sword and cut at me even as I fell.

We were confronted on another unrailed plank bridge between houses, which crossed an alley far below, one of the Back

Streets. It ran from a narrow ledge projecting partway down a higher building to the roof-ridge of a lower one, and a ladder joined it to the higher roof from which we had just descended. I blessed Felkior mentally for his "bladework before footwork" approach as I planted my soles as if taking root, and defended solidly against the Butcher's backswing.

I think he was not expecting me to have much skill, for his first attacks were loose. He soon found, however, that Felkior had drilled me in a solid defence, and his bladework and his concentration tightened as he sought a way to penetrate it. His injury was to his right leg, with which he led, so his stance was solidly supported on his sound left, but he could not strike forward with full power.

We fenced in silence, except for the clang of our weapons and our heavy breathing – his somewhat faster and shallower than mine, which gave me hope of wearing him down. Seeing that he could not break my defence, however, and being at a disadvantage in position – for my back was to a wall as his was not – he began to move backwards along the narrow bridge, drawing me away from the wall. He had noted, I think, the brief horror of my downward glance.

My response was to take two short steps and press my attack, turning his maneuver back against him. Again, I think this surprised him, and he flailed for a couple of strokes, barely defending himself. I let the opportunity go by, however, my lack of quickness allowing him to recover. He was more on his guard now, for he knew he faced an equal, and he probed and tested my defence, but I had learned to keep out Tamas, whose swordsmanship had surpassed that of most of his contemporaries, and I held.

I observed the marks of the wasps which had assailed him; he had been stung on the cheek and on the hands, and his flesh was distorted, red and puffy with reaction to the venom of the insects. He must be in some pain, I thought.

Sweat was starting on his forehead, despite the chill of the morning, and I knew that if I could endure without making mistakes I had won, for he was not my better and I was uninjured. He must have known this too, for he spoke, I think in an attempt to distract me.

"Bass," he said, and his voice was lighter than I had antici-
pated. "What am I to you?"

I did not answer, though I had a flicker of surprise that he
knew my name. Most likely, I thought, he was one of the courtiers
I had met all at once when I was presented to the King, so he re-
members my name though I do not know his.

"Bass," he said again. "Is it because I killed your countryman? It was not for his nationality, for I did not know it."

Still I did not answer.

"He was only a practice piece," continued the murderer, "not
like the others. He meant nothing in particular. Bass," he said,
"what is your price for him?"

I kept silent and concentrated on my fencing.

"Surely," he said, "it is not because of the others. You can
hardly have discovered last night's yet."

So he had killed last night. I fought on with renewed concentration, knowing that I was avenging six poor souls.

"The watchman was only to throw the watch's investigation
into disarray," he continued. "He was nobody."

The man had had a wife, a son, a brother. He had friends,
comrades who mourned him. I set my teeth and fought on.

"The nobleman was just a puppy, a plaything I had tired of,
who knew enough to be a little dangerous. Oh, but it is so much
more satisfying to dispose of them oneself! I will always do that
now." He cut unexpectedly low, but I was concentrating on his
blade, not his words, and parried successfully, almost turning it
into a cut at his injured leg. He fought grimly, without speaking,
until he felt he had regained parity, then talked on.

"The Commissioner fellow, now that was political. He led
opposition against one of my measures. Feeble opposition, and
it would not have succeeded, but still I took pleasure in ending
it and replacing him with someone who would see things *my*
way. It is so important to have people who see things one's own
way. Do you not find?"

The voice had been lightening all this time, and I felt I could
almost place it, but deliberately concentrated on the task at hand.
Block the thrusts. Parry, riposte. Keep the stance firm. Do not
let him force –

Do not let her force you off the edge.

I almost did, as the realisation hit me that I was fighting a woman. For a moment I faltered, and she almost had me, but I beat her blade aside and tried to trap it on her weaker right side. She freed it and stepped back.

"Do you know me, Bass? Do you know me now?" she said, and I did.

It was the Countess after all.

I still said nothing, for it seemed to encourage her to talk, to confess, and I thought it distracted her more than it did me – certainly more than it would distract me to try to talk and fight at the same time. But now that I knew her, she must kill me, not merely escape. I locked my gaze on her, seeking to predict the next movement of her blade, and defended doggedly while looking for a chance to disarm her.

"So now you are wondering why I killed Mende. My faithful servant. Wounded in an attack intended to kill me. My confidante, the companion of my youth. I am hinting to you, Bass. Why do you think I killed her?"

Parry, bind, thrust. I almost had her that time – she was tiring. She was working up to a revelation, I realised, and also losing strength; shortly she would be desperate. I held my stance, parried her attacks and watched for a mistake.

"Did you ever wonder, Bass, where Sallia came from? How Mende ended up with a foster daughter? She is mine, mine and Felkior's, and only Mende knew. And I killed Mende – " she struck hard in punctuation of each panted phrase – "because she would have told – because she had found out – that I had had – her son – Corius – killed."

She had, at last, succeeded in startling me, but my concentration was such that her desperate lunge failed, and I turned it into the opportunity I had been seeking. There was a confused flurry of limbs and weapons, and she went down with a thump at an angle on the narrow catwalk, ankles over one edge, shoulders over the other. There was a clattering sound as her sword hit the cobbles in the alley three stories below, and my blade was steady at her throat.

"It is over, Countess," I told her. "It ends now."

She bit her lip in frustration, casting down her eyes within the domino of the Uncast.

"You have bested me, Bass," she said. "Well done; few have done so in the City of Masks – and none who are living." She clutched at her wounded leg through the skirts of her black cloak. "I will have a limp like Mende, I think. Poor Mende, I am sorry now I killed her. Will you help a lady up?" she asked, extending her left hand, her right still clutching her leg.

I had to lower my sword and direct it to the side in order to grasp her left hand with my left. She pulled her uninjured left leg back beneath her, then thrust hard with it, and there was another confused flurry. She came up fast inside the reach of my sword. I felt a sharp pain in my left side, then there was another thump as I let her go in shock and spun around to protect myself, slipping on the wet wood, flinging her away from me so that she struck the boards again, a glancing blow from which she rebounded, falling from the high bridge as I fell onto it. An iron hand clutched at my winded and wounded stomach. I didn't hear her scream or hit; I was vomiting in shock. I dropped my sword over the edge, and almost passed out, clutching the board so hard that I drove splinters into my hands.

I hung there across the flimsy bridge, feeling the blood seeping out of my side where her dagger point had penetrated through the heavy cloth of my cloak and the braided canvas and leather of Juliana's gift, and realised that without that gift I would undoubtedly be dead.

Unexpectedly, a voice spoke above me. Spoke my name.

"Bass," it said, and it was Bardo's voice. "Bass, are you all right? Did she get you? I saw the dagger flash."

"Winded," I gasped. "Stabbed. Just give me – minute." He hurried down the ladder to me and helped me to drag myself up onto the bridge. It was full light by this time, and I could see the Countess's body lying face-up in the alley below. Bardo made me a pad for my wound out of stuff he evidently carried for such a purpose, doing so with an efficiency that bespoke practice, and had me put pressure on it. When I was sitting with my back against the wall, breathing heavily but in no further danger, he left me and descended to the alley. He did this by crossing the bridge, sliding down the roof to the left to where it ended above a side street, and, so far as I could see, descending a ladder down the side of the building, which clearly he knew of as it was not visible from where I sat. After several minutes he appeared at the head of some stairs leading to the alley from one of the middle streets on my right, having apparently walked around the building.

He descended to the Back Way and checked the Countess's body. "Dead," he called up to me.

I let out a breath I had not realised I was holding, and regretted it when it twinged my injury. Feeling unable to speak, I waved to indicate that I had heard.

"Can you hold on there?" he asked. "It will take me just a minute to fetch help."

I waved my assent, and he disappeared again up the stairs to the street.

I have tired myself thinking of it all again, and though Juliana has not come to confiscate my quill, I think I will leave my narration for the night.

The first of the third month

Today I feel stronger, and I may almost bring my account up to date. My wound is healing well under Juliana's care and that of an apothecary who is one of the priestesses of the Moon. Our office is closed, and for urgent needs the Calarian community must apply to me here at the house. Juliana keeps the door and determines, with ruthless firmness, what qualifies as "urgent", so I have been little troubled. The Calarians, also, seem to respect that I gained my injury in pursuit of their fellow's murderer, and stay away that I may rest and recover.

To return to my story, however. Two of Bardo's large men came up the ladder he had descended, equipped with ropes and tools. They fixed the ropes to the plank bridge, bound me lightly to it, and detached it from its moorings, then lowered it, and me, gently to the alley below, where several others of their comrades received it and bore me away to my own house. They would return, they said, for the offal, by which they intended the Countess. From effective ruler of the City, she had become a corpse in a filthy alley, like her victims.

The apothecary I have mentioned came to me at the instance of Tamas and dosed me so that I slept, and I did not learn of what else had happened until the morrow. I woke to find faithful Corius sitting by the window with a book, which he set down as I stirred and asked him, "What time is it?"

"It is afternoon of the day after Solstice," he told me, "about two or three hours since the noon bell. Are you thirsty?"

I was, and he helped me to drink and with other matters, and I lay back again in the covers feeling as if I had run a race bearing a barrel on my shoulders. My side hurt where the Countess had stabbed me, and it also hurt to breathe. I was much strapped and bandaged under my night clothing.

"You have broken several ribs," said Corius, as he spooned a rich broth into my mouth, "and must stay immobile for a little, until they and the wound in your side have healed. The apothecary says it is a clean wound; the gut is whole, though you have lost blood and you will have a scar always. It was as well Juliana gave you that padded undergarment, or it would have been much worse."

"I know it," I said. "Will you thank her for me?"

"You can thank her yourself," he said, "I will fetch her once you have eaten; she has been awaiting your awakening."

When I had finished the broth and he had wiped my chin, he went out. I heard footsteps and voices and the rustle of her dress, and she stepped into the room and smiled tentatively at me.

"How do you feel?" she asked.

"Weak," I said. I am usually a loquacious man, but the injury to my ribs convinced me as discretion never had, to keep my responses brief. "Alive, however, thanks to your forethought."

"I am very glad of it," she said, and came over to clasp my hand in both of hers, and sit beside me upon the bed. We were silent for a time, I feeling unable to say anything – not only from my injuries, but from reticence, for though I talk and talk, I often do not know what to say in particular situations. What I mean, and what I am expressing badly, is that I, who had almost lost my life – which concentrates a man's mind upon essentials – wished to speak to her of love, and never having had opportunity to do so to any woman previous, I could not think well how to begin.

After a little I saw tears leaking from beneath her mask, and falling to the quilt beside me.

"Juliana," I said, "what is wrong? Did you suffer some loss yesterday?" My first thought was that somehow her father, or perhaps old Felkior, had come to harm and Corius had so far spared me the news.

"Nay," she said softly, "but almost I lost what is most precious to me, and I am weeping because it was so close, and because – because now I have the chance given me again, and I do not know what to say."

I was not clear-headed, what between my injury and the drugs, but perhaps this helped me to see more clearly in some strange way; as when, if you have such an affliction of the eyes as have I, you are more able to remark something large, which others who have better sight may miss amid the detail they can perceive. I explain badly. But what I did was reach out and gather her carefully into my arms, and she wept for a time against my shoulder, awkwardly, for she was tender of my ribs.

"Juliana," I said at last.

"Gregorius," she replied softly.

"The Countess yesterday said a strange thing. I do not know if it was only to distract me. She said that your mother – that she had killed her because she was close to finding out – who had killed her son. Her son Corius."

She stiffened.

"Juliana, tell me, what is this tale?"

"Gregorius," she said, and then in Corius's voice, "Master. It is true. My brother – " she resumed her own voice – "my brother was killed a year ago. We did not know why or by whom. Within his clenched fist was found a scrap of paper, torn from a larger sheet, with part of a name – a name we recognised as belonging to one of the Personalist exiles resident in Calaria.

"I assumed his name, his role, his clothing and his mask, and took ship to Calaria, working my passage as a sailmaker. When I reached the capital I had some difficulty locating the man; the Personalists were suspicious of me, thinking me a spy, and would not speak of him. This increased my own suspicions. At length, however, I discovered that the man had died not long before my brother.

"The trail was cold, and indeed, I think it was a false trail, manufactured by the Countess – evil woman that she was. I realised that I had to return to the City, and at that time I en-

countered Tailor, and learned of your need for a manservant –
Corius's occupation.

"Wanting to preserve my pretence, I applied for the post,
thinking that to be associated with a foreigner would be no bad
thing – for it might give me some protection, and access to other
avenues of inquiry. Tailor characterised you as a kindly man
but – not subtle, and I did not fear that you would find me out.
And it was so; I presented to you a manservant and you saw a
manservant. Forgive me, Master, for my deception."

"Hush," said I, "it was not with malice toward me. But did
you plan to tell me? Even just now, you continued in the deception."

"Oh, Master – "

"Gregorius."

"Gregorius, I would have told you when you were well. For
I could hardly keep up the pretence indefinitely; at some time
you would have expected to see both Juliana and Corius in the
same room. But as Corius I could take care of you as Juliana
could not."

I thought of the assistance "Corius" had rendered me not an
hour previously, and blushed. She laughed.

"My dear Gregorius, think of me in the manner of a nurse,"
she said.

"Is this another mask?" I asked.

"If you like," she said. "But I am glad you have seen through
the deception, for now I can be with you as myself. I know Gregorius well, for I have been with him in all situations, day and
night, and observed him when he was in all his moods; and besides, Gregorius, there is no guile in you, whoever sees you sees
the whole man. You might be a model for my father's sermon of
wearing the mask of one's own face. But you do not know Juliana; you know only Corius, and Corius is rather more serious
and grim than Juliana. Perhaps it is being dead that does it."

I could not but laugh, and at once regretted it, for when one's
ribs are broken laughter is ill-advised. She was at once contrite,
apologised and fetched the apothecary's preparation, which she
insisted upon feeding me; I could not resist, and slipped again
into sleep.

I awoke after dark to find Juliana asleep, curled up beside
me on the covers like a cat. I tried to slip from the bed without

waking her, but could not, and she assisted me in her role as nurse and fed me a little broth again. I drifted off with her lying beside me, holding my hand. This contented me greatly, and I thought to say to her that I would always have it so, but sleep overtook me before I found the energy to speak.

The next day was much the same, as I restored my blood with sleep and rich broth, Juliana tending me devotedly. I asked her of Tamas and Felkior, and she replied, "They are both well, and younger than I have seen them; their adventure has done them great good, I think. If you are stronger tomorrow I will have them in, and they can tell you of it."

I was stronger on the morrow – the twenty-seventh of the second month – and Juliana sent a messenger for the old men, who came clattering up the stairs, laughing and chattering like a pair of schoolboys. Juliana hushed them severely and led them, chastened but still exchanging conspiratorial glances and chuckles, into my sickroom.

"So you have penetrated my daughter's deception," said Tamas when we had greeted one another gladly. They sat on chairs Juliana had placed at the foot of the bed; she sat in one beside my head and clasped my hand tightly as was now her custom.

"I hope that is all – " began Felkior jocularly, but a swift nudge in his ribs from his friend conveyed the glare which Juliana had turned upon him, and he fell silent, his schoolboy jest uncompleted.

"Yes," I said, "though she was a most convincing young man and a good servant, yet I prefer her in her own person. And did you protect her adequately when you took her among the dangers of the Temple?"

"According to the Temple," Felkior quibbled, "it was not her we took. Though that may change, perhaps."

"Felkior," she said, "we can speak of that later. Gregorius wants to hear the story of our adventures in the Temple, for all he knows is that we succeeded in substituting ourselves for Uncle Benor and his catamite – I mean, acolyte."

For all her fierceness to them, she had the sense of humour and fun which Corius lacked, and as they told the story – much of which I have already related – she laughed even as she chided them: "Oh, Father, you exaggerate shamefully! I did not wrestle with the acolyte, he hardly struggled, the little coward. All the resistance had been long beaten out of him. All I had to do was tackle him." Or: "Well, of course we could not have stolen the Sunmask, you never meant that seriously, did you? Benor knew who we were – we would never have got away with something like that. Tying him and his acolyte up and preaching a substitute sermon could be seen as a prank, but stealing the Sunmask would be a serious crime. Besides, I thought it would create more confusion if I kicked it among the priests – nothing like gold among priests to cause a scramble."

After the release of the wasps, Juliana – or rather, Corius – and Tamas had withdrawn into the Temple as expeditiously as possible to avoid any crossbow bolts and hurried to the small office where alms were received and counted. There they had removed the Archpriest's outer robes and mask, and reversed their inner robes and assumed the character of ordinary priests. By this time the other priests had fled into the Temple also, and they mingled with this crowd and escaped in the confusion back to the Archpriest's quarters.

Felkior had had what he professed to be an uninteresting time there, as the prisoners had wisely not attempted anything. They had loosened the cords on the acolyte's wrists so that he could eventually escape the bindings and assist his master, but left his blindfold and gag in place; they had then vanished through the secret passage, locking and barring it carefully behind them, and returned to the bordello.

They found the mistress there slightly concerned, for one of her girls – the very one we had observed exiting from the establishment when we had approached it – had not returned from her early call. "It is a holiday, though," she observed, "and perhaps the young man is making a day of it. Provided that he pays, he is welcome to. But one of her regulars has asked for her, and said he had arranged with her to visit today, and it is not like her to be tardy. One worries, with all this talk of murderers about."

The blood of the three being up after their successful foray, they naturally volunteered to search for the young woman to see if she might have come to harm. The mistress remembered the general layout of the map that had been handed in, and this gave them a direction to search, off to the side of the temple district – the possibility of encountering Bardo's men out for vengeance only adding spice for three who were masked as Young Felkior.

Sadly, they found her, the Butcher's sixth victim, and had since put together a theory. "She was in figure and face, though not in the colouring of her hair, very like the Countess," said Juliana. "It is not unlikely that they were related, given the habits of past Counts. She was employed on the night of the previous murder to go to approximately the area where that crime occurred, and had returned smelling of expensive perfume and saying that it was 'easy money'. We think the Countess used her as what is known here as a dummy or placeholder. Sometimes when a person must be seen to be in one place but has reasons – such as another identity – for being elsewhere at the time, a placeholder is employed who appears enough like the principal to pass in their mask. I have done it myself once or twice with Sallia, so that Juliana could be seen at the same time as Corius. She is much of my size if you bind her bosom firmly, and she is capable of being silent for as much as half an hour, though I would not try her longer."

"So this girl was a placeholder for the Countess to divert suspicion from her?" I asked.

"That is what we think," said Tamas. "Between the chaos engendered in the Watch's investigation by the death of the watchman, the breaking of the pattern centred around the old Coslian Manor, and the fact that the Countess had been seen by many witnesses at the time of the murder to be elsewhere, she might have continued her career for far longer, had it not been for your quick-witted observation and courage."

I waved away this undeserved compliment.

"But the weakness in her plan, of course, was the girl," Juliana continued. "A secret known to a living person is no secret. Hence she became the next victim."

"And not a priest, as we had speculated," said Tamas.

"Indeed, though doubtless she would have worked her way around to the priests before long. We may have saved Uncle Benor from assassination more than once, for she despised him – despised all men of his kind, for she had one less means to control them."

"And what of Benor? Have his experiences been mentioned? Has he sought any vengeance?" I asked.

"Officially, it was Benor who gave the sermon at Solstice," said Tamas with some amusement, "something which must gall him exceedingly, particularly as several people, I hear, have said publicly that it was far better than his usual sermons. No doubt he holds a personal grudge, but that hardly changes matters between us; I did him no physical harm, and his embarrassment was not public. He probably thinks that we performed the whole exercise in order to preach the sermon, though the wasps may puzzle him."

"The wasps," I said. "Has Bardo said anything?"

They exchanged glances. "Bardo has had other matters on his mind," said Tamas. "The death of the Countess has left a gaping hole in the power structure of the City, as if in the bottom of a ship, and a number of assassinations and attempted assassinations have occurred among those rushing in to fill the hole. Bardo's men have been formed into a militia company 'to keep public order', and the wise among the powerful are keeping within doors until the situation calms down. The upper levels of the City are at a standstill; the Commissioners of Masks have not met, nor has the Royal Council, and the Sunpriests are quieter than I have known them – though they have the additional cause that they were severely embarrassed by the fiasco of the Solstice Ceremony."

"The ordinary commerce of the City, though, goes on as usual," said Felkior, "if a little nervously at first, when the quarrels of the nobles looked like spilling onto the streets. Bardo's men do not harrass ordinary citizens, they mount no raids, they merely stand on street corners, well armed and grim-looking, and glare at any one who seems about to start an argument. All of them have those seamen's whistles now, and if one blows his whistle others will come running."

"I have seen twenty of them converge inside half a minute to separate two nobles having a squabble," said Tamas. "They did not beat the nobles, though – they are well disciplined – just sent them on their way in opposite directions. I think they may be foreign mercenaries Bardo has hired, for on the few occasions I have heard one speak, his accent has not been that of the City."

"So Bardo is in effective control of the City?" I asked.

"Yes, and he has said nothing to us, so it seems he is not upset with us for our interference in his plans. You did him a great favour, Bass, in killing the Countess, and I think he is grateful."

"You did us all a great favour, and we are all grateful," said Juliana. "But she did you no favours, and we ought not to tire you, you are looking pale again. Nay, Father, you and Felkior must go, and I will feed Mysir Bass a little bread dipped in broth, and then he must sleep."

"Mysir Bass again, is it?" joked Tamas, "I thought it was Gregorius now. I go, I go!" – for she was hurrying them to the door like a farm woman herding her hens. "Have him to yourself, daughter, but remember, he is delicate!" he called as she closed the door behind them, and I heard Felkior make some joke about "delicacy", and their laughter descending the stairs.

Juliana fussed around me adjusting my pillows and then told me to lie quiet while she went and heated the broth. I was smiling when she returned and she asked me what I was thinking.

"I was thinking," I said, "that I hope I can take it with as much humour as the old men, when you are fierce with me instead of on my behalf."

"Oh, hush," she said, but she was smiling. "Eat your broth."

That was the twenty-seventh. There is little to say of the three days since; I have written this journal, eaten more each day (today a full meal, and not invalids' broth, but honest beefsteak – for Juliana's apothecary recommends beef for strengthening the blood after a wound), and, of course, talked with Juliana.

Tomorrow I hope to spend time out of bed, for my inactivity is galling to me now that I am awake for longer. Juliana has taken to reading to me, old tales of chivalry mostly, and I lie and listen to her voice with pleasure. Whenever she reads the words "gentle knight" she chuckles and looks at me with such a loving smile I cannot but smile in return.

(Later). The old men visited again this afternoon. The political situation is unchanged, but they are expecting Bardo to make some announcement shortly. They spoke of the Countess and how she terrorised the city.

"She, herself, had suffered," I pointed out.

"Mysir, you are too good," said Tamas. "You read our play, every word of which was true. Indeed, she tried to kill you, also. Many people suffer, but if they all inflicted their suffering on others again, the world would be in worse case even than it is. The Countess was a snake, and you need not kiss a snake to treat it fairly, as the saying is."

"I have always wondered, though," said his old friend, "if she might have gone a different way if I had spoken to her differently that time."

"And I have always thought," said Tamas, "that she would not. She had set her foot upon her path before you knew her. If you must blame another, blame the Count her father; but he is to blame for his choices only. She is to blame for hers."

Felkior clasped his friend's shoulder silently in thanks, and they left, much more sobered than they had come.

The second of the third month

I have much to write of this afternoon, for this morning brought an unexpected summons.

I had awoken early, almost at my usual hour, and with Juliana's help had dressed and was eating with her at the table. We were discussing – or rather, arguing genially over – when I might return to the office, when a knock came at the door upon the ground level which gives upon the stairs up to our quarters. She at once transformed herself to Corius – something she can do with remarkable rapidity, for she wears his clothing beneath hers, and has only to cast off her outer dress, tie back her hair and change masks – and ran down to answer it.

It was a messenger, and the missive he left was addressed in both our names – that is, Gregorius Bass and Corius his servant, for we had not advertised abroad that Juliana was living in my quarters. Not that our behaviour together was in any way improper, but that I did not wish her reputation impugned, and she did not wish questions to be raised regarding the whereabouts of Corius.

I opened the letter, and she leaned against my shoulder to read it with me. She reads rather more rapidly than do I, and drew in her breath before I had well got past the salutation.

"Master," she said, which it is her habit still to call me while in the guise of Corius, "what do you think this means?"

I finished reading to the foot of the page – it was not a long note, and the import of it was clear: we were summoned that day to appear before the King. "I cannot think," I said. "It may be good news or bad. Good, I hope, but perhaps I am to be tried for slaying the Countess."

"Surely not," she said, but looked concerned. "Bardo would not permit it."

"Do you think Bardo in control of the King?" I asked.

"Bardo is in control of the whole city," she replied.

The summons was for later that morning. "Time enough," she said, checking it again upon the paper, "to shave you, and for us both to wash and change. I will do the shaving, for your hand shakes yet."

"I, however, will do the washing," I insisted.

"What, of me as well? I own that it is only fair, as payback for my washing you all this week," said the mischief. I shook my finger at her, speechless and blushing, for I own that the image... well.

"Not? Ah, well, perhaps some future time," she said, unrepentant. "Come, Master, I will heat the water and do you choose the clothing you will wear."

"What should I be?" I asked, meaning, what mask.

"How is the letter addressed? 'To the Gentle Knight Gregorius Bass, and Corius, his manservant.' It is not as the Envoy that he would speak with you, nor yet, it seems, as the Innocent Man."

That disquieted me a little, but there was nothing I could do. While the water heated (Juliana had a fine instinct for getting it to the right temperature), she descended to the street and sent one of the urchins who carry messages to bring a sedan-chair in time for me to be carried to the Palace.

I had already my Gentle Knight mask on when she came to shave me – I had been wearing rather the smaller and more comfortable mask of the Innocent Man during my convalescence – and Juliana seemed hesitant.

"What is it?" I asked.

"Master," she said – for she was still Corius – "your mask. I cannot shave you properly with it in place." I had not considered this, and was lifting my hands to remove it when she, eyes squeezed shut, halted me with a gesture and the word "Nay!".

"Juliana, what is the matter?" I asked.

"Oh, Master, you are such a foreigner still sometimes!" she remonstrated. "First, I am currently Corius – do not forget while we are in the Palace and call me by the wrong name! And secondly, you were about to remove your mask before me, as if it were your shirt."

"Well, and you have seen me without my shirt many a time, and my trousers, too, and it did not seem to concern you," I protested.

"But this is your *mask*, Master," she said, as to a child. "Please, turn aside, replace it with the Innocent Man – which indeed you are currently portraying! – and I will explain as I shave you."

I did so, and when she had lathered me and was scraping the blade along my cheek, she said, "Master, in this City, even many lovers do not see one another without masks. There is even a saying: Lovers who go unmasked together are all naked."

I waited until she had removed the blade, and replied, "Your pardon, Ju – Corius. I see I have offended you without meaning to. Please forgive me."

"Oh, Master, of course I forgive you; you meant no harm. But please, try to think like a Bonvidaeoan while you are here. Even the Innocent Man is not the Innocent Man any more if he takes off his mask, after all; he is only a naked man."

She left me alone to wash, as I did her, and when she had dressed in Corius's best clothes she came to help me with the last tidying of my clothing. I asked her something which I had thought of in the meantime.

"Corius, tell me, when you were in Calaria, how was it to be surrounded by people with no masks?"

"Can you imagine yourself in one of those remote regions," she said, "where it is said that the savages wear no clothing – only perhaps a string of beads?"

"I would not know where to look."

"Indeed. But I adapted; it is only different customs, and though I have been raised in this City and so its customs are a part of me, I was able to think that these people were not setting out to offend me; they were innocents who saw no harm in walking around without a mask. Indeed, as a Personalist I approved it. I could not look them in the face, though," she confessed.

"I remember now at first I thought you shifty, for you would not look me in the face," I said. "But once I had the mask on you did, and soon we were in Bonvidaeo and all was new, and I thought no more about it."

I leaned upon her a little going down the stairs, for my wound still pulled, though it was beginning to itch, and the apothecary said that was good, and a sign that it was healing. At the bottom waited the sedan chair.

She helped me climb in, and would have walked beside it, but one of the large men who were the bearers said to her genially, "Eh, lad, hop in, art only a little lad," and she joined me, facing backward as I faced forward. She leaned over and whispered to me, "Bardo's mercenaries," having apparently recognised the accent to which her father had alluded.

They carried us quickly and efficiently, with the curtains drawn closed, to the Palace, where we had to hand out our summons for inspection by the Guard – more large men of a similar appearance. We were waved through, and the bearers took us all the way inside and to a small room which was opened by a functionary (we heard his voice). There we were permitted to exit the conveyance, and found Tamas and Felkior, who had received a summons for the same hour. We had just begun to speculate when another functionary opened the opposite door and told us, "His Grace the King will see you now."

We filed into a room which was evidently an informal reception room, rather than the throne room I had been received in previously. At the head of a table, no bigger than a large kitchen-table, sat a stocky man in good, but not ostentatious robes and a mask of considerably less artifice than the confection I had seen just over two months previously.

"Greetings," he said, "will you not sit down?" – gesturing me to his right and Tamas to his left. Juliana-Corius sat to my right and Tamas guided Felkior to the fifth chair, on his left. The functionary left us alone.

"Well, Bass, I am glad to see you so recovered," said the man at the table's head, and something about how he said my name, or his smile, brought recognition.

"Bardo?" I said. "Do you call yourself King now?"

"Oh, I have been *called* King for a long time," he said, "but now I am taking Holy Tamas's sermon to heart, and have become King in truth. Indeed, I think I will be known as King Bardo now. It is my given name," he added in an aside. "I am weary of this whole Emilion nonsense. In fact, now that I think on it my father and his grandfather had also the given name of Bardo, so I am Bardo the Third. I might as well rewrite the history of the last three hundred years; I have been rewriting the history of the past week, and have found it a rewarding occupation."

We were all stunned into silence for a few moments.

"Well," said Tamas at length, "that explains how you were able to command the resources to hire so many foreign mercenaries. Your Grace," he added.

"Indeed," the King replied with a small smile. "But foreign mercenaries, as any student of history such as our good friend the Keeper will assure you, are not a long-term solution to any political situation. You gentlemen, on the other hand, may well be such a solution.

"My problem," he went on, "was that my ancestors, beginning with that drunkard Emilion, had made a hole in the vessel which held their power and allowed it to leak out. It was not allowed, however, to lie upon the ground. People like the Countess – and, sadly, there have been several people like the Countess in the history of our city, though she is undoubtedly the worst – have been extremely careful to pick it up, and put it in other vessels which would not spill so readily.

"Hence the Commissioners of Masks, the Royal Council, and indeed the Priests of the Sun. It would seem to an observer that the Priests held least power of all of these, since they had only one voice – the Archpriest – who by virtue of his office served upon both the other bodies, where he was often a minority opinion. However, by the doctrine of Characterism, propagated through the priests, the Commissioners held their power; and the Royal Council picked up any scraps that the Commissioners left, like the dogs that they generally are."

"Hence your adoption of the Personalist cause," suggested Felkior.

"Hence, as you say. Do not mistake me, I hold Personalism to be true as well as useful – indeed, useful because it is true. But it also formed what I saw as a means to an end. By bringing open conflict within the City, I hoped to create a situation in which I could weigh in with my foreign mercenaries on the Personalist side, stage a revolution, and depose the Commissioners – keeping myself, naturally, as a puppet king. I see now that your advice was good, and that this would have been a disaster for the City, but it was the only way I could think of to overcome the incumbent disaster."

"Do you refer now to the Countess?" asked Felkior, who appeared to be the only one of us still possessing the power of speech.

"Ha. Yes, primarily I do," replied His Grace. "The problem with the Countess was this: Every man in the City feared her, all the wise and half the foolish hated her, and all the foolish and half the wise were in love with her. Or so I thought, but it seems that Mysir Bass fell into a category of his own."

He looked at me inquiringly and I sought for an answer.

"When I pursued her," I temporised, "I did not know she was the Countess."

"But when you defeated her, you did," he said. "I was there, remember, I heard the whole thing. My apologies, by the way, for not intervening, but it looked to me all along as if you were going to win, and I thought that if I interrupted I would be as likely to distract you as her, since I would be coming from behind you. Ah," he said, "I should be honest; I was afraid of her too. As you, apparently, were not, or else you are a man of great courage."

"I was not particularly afraid," I said; "she was not as strong as me and had been wounded, you see, and I could see that she was not a better fencer."

"Yes, Bass, but no other man in the City would have thought that way. It would have been: 'Oh, gods, this is the *Countess*! I am a dead man standing up.' We have an expression for that in the City; it is called 'putting on the mask of the defeated'."

"Do you mean to say, Your Grace," said Tamas suddenly, "that you knew it was the Countess before Bass did?"

"Oh, I had known it was the Countess for some time. When I discounted her as being the Butcher to you, it was only to keep you from doing anything foolish like stalking her. But I had to catch her being the Butcher, you see; then I could arrest the Butcher, and try the Butcher, and execute the Butcher – or perhaps just execute, there was too much risk in the other two –

and, oh, has anyone seen the Countess lately? Oh, look, the Butcher was a woman. Oh, what a coincidence. Dear me."

"I seem to recall you saying she was sane," I said, "Your Grace."

"You need not Grace me every time, you know," he said, "I am off my dignity here. My dear Bass, that was most definitely a lie. Nobody as vicious as the Countess could possibly be sane. Look at how she attacked you at the end. I can be ruthless enough, as you know, but I know that there have to be rules. If I am duelling with a man and he disarms me fairly and has his sword at my throat, I give up – for then. I may try again against him later, but for then, he has beaten me and I surrender. I do not try to knife him after asking him to help me up. That was the Countess's whole trouble; she thought the rules did not apply to her. She just did whatever vicious thing she thought of, and expected all the consequences to fall on other people. Sooner or later, somebody with that kind of thinking is going to run up against reality coming in the other direction, and then she will suddenly be lying dead in an alley full of sewage."

There was something of an uncomfortable pause after this analysis, and the King seemed to sense it, for he changed his topic. "In any case, Bass, I owe you my gratitude. Which is odd, if you think on it, for if my Envoy to Calaria killed a powerful member of the nobility – even one that everybody hated and feared – Calaria would probably declare war on us."

I must have looked worried, for he said, "Come now, Bass, fear not. You have the good fortune to be in Bonvidaeo now, not Calaria. And in Bonvidaeo, you were not the Envoy when you fought her, and she was not the Countess, and so no such charge can be made. Besides which, it is quite legal to duel here, and she broke the rules, and you kept them, so whatever happened to her is her own fault. And furthermore – and this is my favourite part – I am the King, and I could pardon you regardless. So thank you, Bass, very much." He even stood up and shook my hand.

"My gratitude will take a more substantial form presently, but first I have some offers of position to make. Felkior."

"Your Grace."

"It has long been an anomaly of the Commission of Masks that the Keeper of the Book is its servant, rather than its master.

It is in Our mind to rectify this situation. What say you, Master Keeper?"

"What would this mastery involve, Your Grace?"

"As I am sure you are aware, it would involve a judicious purge of certain elements in the Commission, and a realignment of its policy to accord more closely with the policy of the Crown."

"I am not a politician, Your Grace."

"Well, do not refuse me yet until you have heard my next offer. Tamas."

"Your Grace."

"I find I am in need of good advice. As I have been the recipient of your good advice previously, and have ignored it to my woe, I wish to appoint you Principal Counsellor – or I should say, We wish to do so – for I would sooner have you with me than against me. What say you?"

"May I offer what counsel I wish without fear of any fate worse than dismissal?"

"You may."

"May I point out to Your Grace those occasions upon which Your Grace failed to act upon my counsel, to Your Grace's woe?"

Bardo laughed hugely. "You may. It would be much less interesting otherwise."

"Then I accept."

"Very good. Your first act as my Principal Counsellor shall be to advise me upon the resolution of the Characterist-Personalist situation. It is in Our mind to effect a conversion of the state from a Characterist to a Personalist position."

"It is my advice that you do not do so."

"And why?"

"Because it is not necessary. Consider this. If you simply repeal the laws against Personalism, and require the Temple to cease to persecute Personalists, then immediately, Characterism begins to wither, and indeed, so does the power of the Commission."

"How so?"

"Because you have admitted the thought that there is the man, and there is the mask, and the two are distinct. Characterism absolutely depends upon denying this, and the Commission's power is only absolute if control of the masks means control of the people. Once allow the people to think of themselves as distinct from their masks, and the Commission's authority is upon their souls no longer."

"Aht, aht, aht – " Felkior said, unable even to begin to articulate his disagreement with this logic.

"Master Keeper, are you about to argue with my Principal Counsellor?" said the King.

"Why, yes," he replied, surprised.

"Then should you not do so as the Lord Keeper of the Book of Masks, the leader of the Commission?"

Felkior's jaw worked.

"Very well, you may closet yourself with my Principal Counsellor and discuss recommendations for the future structure of the Council and Commission. Abolish them both, for all I care, and set up something new in their stead. I will be at your disposal when you have deliberated – send word through any liveried man. Ask them for lunch when you want it – no, I had better send it in," he said, clearly realising that once the two old friends began their debate they would not cease for such an irrelevance as nourishment. "Through that door and the next, we do not want to hear your shouting. Go, go. Oh, and Felkior?"

"Your Grace?"

"I suggest that it would be appropriate to grant Tamas a Character. Bass too, of course. Oh, and – whose idea were the wasps?"

"Mine, your Grace," said a small voice to my right.

"I thought as much, they had a Corian ring to them somehow. Corius as well, then. Off you go, good, good," he said, standing and closing the door after them. We could hear them debating beyond it already until they crossed the next chamber and closed its door in turn.

The King rang for a man and arranged for lunch to be sent to the old men at midday, then turned to us again.

"Now. Rewards. I must say, I like this approach to monarchy much better than the other," he remarked. "Bass, have you given any thought to your future?"

"Some, Your Grace, but I have been unwell these past few days," I said.

"In Our service, too, or at least so We choose to construe it," he said. "Which leads me to my offer. I believe We have need of a loyal, experienced Envoy to represent Us in Calaria – some reliable person who knows the country, has contacts in the diplomatic service there, and so forth. Do you think you would be available?"

I was so astonished that I did not know what to say. "Your Grace," I answered at last, "I – the way bristles with difficulties. I am not even sure that I am permitted to discuss such an offer – it may be treason to even consider it."

"Come, come, surely not treason?" he said. "I am not asking you to be my spy, Bass, only my Envoy."

"Indeed, Your Grace, but I think my conditions of employment specifically forbid me from entering into the employ of foreign nations, not only during but also after my term of service. I – am most flattered, Your Grace, for I am little regarded in my own country, and indeed, that would hinder me in representing you even were it not forbidden me. But I must in honesty decline."

"My dear Bass, you do all things in honesty, and it is for this reason that I wished to employ you. But come, I will not press you if it is against your principles, that would be to mar what I most value in you. At least it is not forbidden you to accept honours from other nations, though? I understand that this is done sometimes?"

"It is done occasionally, yes, with the permission of my sovereign – " I began.

"Then as soon as I can obtain the permission of your sovereign I will make you Sir Gregorius Bass, for you make far too good a Gentle Knight not to be a knight in truth. And in the message I send to your superior – Waters?"

"Rivers, Your Grace."

"Rivers, I will emphasize the considerable service you have rendered to the city of Bonvidaeo in assisting us in our actions against a notorious criminal, whose first known victim was a man of your own nation. Happening to be in a position to pursue this criminal, you did so without hesitation and with a commendable grasp of the situation. Through your swift, decisive and above all courageous actions, in the course of which you were most unfortunately wounded by the criminal in question, this fearsome threat to the good order of our city has now been removed, and both the citizens and government of Bonvidaeo, and the Calarian citizens here resident, have expressed their considerable gratitude. Indeed, I think they may well express it in the form of a spontaneous collection for a tribute to be presented to you. I shall suggest it," and he made a note. "Naturally this will lead to warmer and closer relations between our state and the nation which you represent, and so on, and so forth."

"Thank you, Your Grace," I said, "I am overwhelmed." I was. Perhaps, I thought, My Lord would at last be pleased with something I had done.

"Now, Corius," said the King, and turned his gaze on my companion, who sat suddenly straight and quivered to be so addressed.

"Come, come, man, you have spoken to me often enough when I was a plotter or a porter. Am I frightening suddenly, now that I am the King?"

"I think, Your Grace," I said, "he may still be worried that you resent the incident of the wasps."

At this, Bardo threw his head back and laughed, a bluff, merry laugh that rang through the room. "But the wasps were *brilliant*!" he exclaimed. "I wish I had thought of the wasps. I had perhaps fifty mercenaries there, but you defeated them with fifteen hundred. Or however many wasps it was. My gods, if I went around punishing intelligence and initiative and courage and loyalty, I would deserve to end up like the Countess. Besides, although I know kings do such things, punishing one's brother-in-law would likely lead to marital difficulties."

"Y-your Grace?"

"Oh, call me Bardo, man, in private. Yes, we are to be relatives – at least, a kind of relative, for though you and Sallia are not blood kin you are as good as. I have asked her, and she has accepted me."

"As Bardo?" asked Corius. "Or as the King?"

He smiled. "Both," he said, "and in that order. I cannot keep my identity secret much longer, for now I have told Sallia it will be discussed in every boudoir in the City before nightfall. I had better hurry with the proclamation, or the news will fall quite flat."

"But Your Grace," I asked, "will the people accept – "

"The people," he said, "will do as they're told. And even if not, she is, of course, the heir general to the Countess – some-

thing which I revealed to her between her first and second faints
– and so eminently suitable as my consort. I do love her, you
know," he said to Corius, I thought a little anxiously; "of all of it,
that at least was not pretence."

"I believe you," said Corius softly.

"Ha, but I cannot have a brother-in-law who is a servant, can
I?" the King went on. "I believe Tamas has acknowledged you
as his?"

Corius nodded.

"Formally?"

"Not formally."

"Hmm, well, a writ of acknowledgement from your father,
countersigned by Us, will suffice for that. I had best get one
from Felkior for Sallia, as well," he said, making another note.
"Which brings us to the subject of your grandfather's title. I
think Tamas may still be technically debarred, especially if he
is reinstated as a Sunpriest, which is one of my intentions, but
you are quite eligible as an acknowledged bastard – which term
I mean merely in a technical sense, of course." He grinned. "So
if you want it, you can be Lord Corius Grantior, Baron Grantior.
Though I think I will make you adopt a wasp as your emblem."

Corius considered, head bowed. At length, he looked up
and said, "If I do not want it, can my sister have it?"

"Juliana? Certainly," said the King, a little surprised; "though
it is not customary for a woman to hold a title when she has
a qualified male relative living, I do not think there is a law
against it. But I would like to do somewhat for you also."

Corius was smiling now. "Then there *is* something you have
not found out." He reached up and undid his hair, allowing it
to fall around his shoulders, reached into his pocket and pulled
out Juliana's mask, and slipped it on. "You see," she said in her
own voice, "what you do for me, you *do* do for my brother also."

The King was a picture of astonishment. Then he roared
with the loudest peal of laughter yet, laughed and laughed until
tears were running down his face and he was pounding the table. I was beginning to fear that he would have a seizure when
he settled down, wiped the moisture from underneath his mask,
and coughed to cleared his throat. "Ahh," he said, "that was
worth two baronies, at least. One for each of you," and he chuck-

led again. "Twins! I should have thought. But was there ever a Corius? I am sure that Sallia spoke as if there was."

Juliana sobered, and looked down. I spoke up for her. "He was one of the Countess's victims," I said. "We are still not sure why. But she had him killed a year ago."

"Condemn that woman," muttered the King, "her list of victims is longer than her legs. Well, now that she is marrying me, I am sure Sallia will not need all the Countess's estates; we can settle one or two on you as some form of compensation, though gods know, it is little enough for a lost brother. I daresay I have a spare title or two as well, if you want them. In fact," he said, "why not tell *me* what *you* want – call it reward, compensation, rightful inheritance, we can work out the details later. Hey?"

"There is one thing I want, but it is not yours to give me," said Juliana. "It is in the gift of Mysir Bass."

I looked at her.

"If you mean my love, it is yours already," I said.

"And shall I then be your leman?" she asked me pertly.

"Oh," I said. "Juliana, will you marry me?"

"Certainly I will," she said, and leaning forward, kissed me. "Now that I have secured a dowry."

The King had a bemused look on his face, which he rubbed, but he was smiling. "Astonishing woman," he said. "She certainly keeps astonishing *me*. Keep hold of her, Bass. And keep her where you can see her – if you can." He clasped my hand again in congratulation.

"Your Grace," Juliana said formally, "all this has been most gratifying, not so say relieving, but my – husband-to-be is not a well man. He still tires easily, and since he will not say anything – being, as he is, courteous in all things – it falls to me to speak on his behalf."

"Oh, very well," said the King, "take him home, and take care of him – he is a treasure of the realm."

"I know it," she said, and smiled.

She is smiling now, standing in the doorway as I write. I will put down the pen, and go to her.

Private journal of Darion, Lord Rivers, Under-secretary to the Foreign Minister of Calaria

The fifth of the third month

That idiot Bass has caught himself up in some condemned intrigue in that city. The King writes that he is pleased with him – a new King, apparently, there are rumours of a coup. I only hope that Bass has not become caught up in local politics, even if he has come out upon what is currently the winning side. That is positively the last thing we need.

He is marrying a Baroness, of all things. It really is most worrying – is she a bribe? Was that what lay behind his clumsy attempt to make me send him money, or fund guards, or whatever he was trying to do? This business of a "criminal" that he killed – was that someone upon the other side whom the new King has criminalized in retrospect?

It worries me exceedingly, and I shall be recalling him and asking him to account for his actions at some length.

Private journal of Sallia

Not dated

Well at last the waiting and all my work has paid off Bardo has proposed and confessed to me who he is and I pretended to faint. And very fortunately myser Bass has killed Mother my real mother and so that is all right I can say now in my journal I always hated her but I never dared to say that even to myself in my head hardly in case she found out that I knew and killed me. I have come into my inheritance and I am to be qeen and even Juliana will be married to myser Bass she is so happy she is so plain poor girl she thought she would never have a lover and myser Bass is kind even if he is not good looking like Bardo or powerful or clever.

I am to be qeen I like writing that.